Susan Carlisle's love affair with books began in the sixth grade, when she made a bad grade in mathematics. Not allowed to watch TV until she'd brought the grade up, Susan filled her time with books. She turned her love of reading into a passion for writing, and now has over ten Medical Romances published through Mills & Boon. She writes about hot, sexy docs and the strong women who captivate them. Visit SusanCarlisle.com.

NURSE TO FOREVER MUM

SUSAN CARLISLE

MILLS & BOON

To Anna, the niece who is so much like me.

I love you.

CHAPTER ONE

"LIZZY, HONEY. STAY STILL." Dr. Cody Brennan squatted on his heels in the hallway in front of the day-care suite to re-tie his daughter's hair-bow. He couldn't keep his frustration out of his voice as he fumbled at forming a loop with the slick ribbon. Suturing he'd learned in medical school, not securing bows.

"Dadd-yyy, it has to be right," Lizzy's whine echoed off the hallway built of glass.

"Hey, mind if I give it a try?" a sweet-sounding feminine voice beside him asked.

Cody looked over his shoulder. Two large, sympathetic green eyes with thick dark lashes met his gaze.

"Dadd-*yyy*," Lizzy moaned.

Not giving him a choice, the woman moved in close. A hint of peach tickled his nose as she tugged the ribbon from his hand, hers brushing over his. With a quick side step he moved aside, giving her better access to Lizzy's ponytail.

As if by magic Lizzy went statue still and the woman in a deft twirl of fingers secured the bow.

"There you go," she announced with such fanfare that she might have been giving Lizzy an award.

"Thanks," he muttered.

Lizzy pulled on his hand. "Let's go, Daddy."

"You need to tell the lady thank you first." He used his stern father voice.

"Thank you." Lizzy obeyed with uncharacteristic shyness.

"No problem." The woman smiled.

The beautiful upturn of her mouth captivated him. Her full lips surrounded white straight teeth, creating a unique sunbeam that pulled him toward her, making him feel good. A sensation he'd not experienced in a long time.

Lizzy tugged on his hand again. Seeing she had regained his attention, she towed him into day care. When he walked out a few minutes later he looked for the woman. There was no one in sight. She'd been wearing a knit top and jeans, so she must be making an early morning patient visit. Why she had grabbed his attention so, he couldn't fathom.

He'd been off women for what seemed like ages now and that suited him fine. After the years of anguish and constant distress his ex-wife Rachael had put them through, his children and he had finally found contentment. Throughout his life he had admired his parents' marriage.

He'd always wanted one like theirs but that dream had been destroyed by the reality of a wife struggling with a drug addiction. Supporting her and raising two small children while at the same time completing his medical training had made him want to find a simpler life. Moving to Maple Island had given him that. It had taken years but he now had the peace he'd hoped for and the ability to give his girls the attention and security they deserved.

Bringing someone into their world would only disrupt what he had so carefully built.

After a car accident, his ex-wife had become hooked on painkillers. He seen the signs, had done everything he could think of to try to help Rachael. She had gone in and out of rehabilitation but nothing had seemed to work. Life had become a round of clinics, counseling, begging and shouting. After finding one of his prescription pads missing, he'd known the crisis Rachael had created had to end. He'd finally accepted defeat. Their marriage was over. He had the girls to consider. Unable to save Rachael, he had to think of Jean and Lizzy and his own sanity.

He'd filed for divorce and full custody. With years' worth of documentation against Rachael, her parental rights had been permanently revoked. Being a solitary parent and a surgeon with a demanding job hadn't been part of his life plan, yet here he was.

Soon after the custody trial he'd met Alex and the answer to his problem had been born. Every day he was grateful for that serendipitous bar conversation he'd had with Dr. Alex Kirkland about the perils and the pitfalls of solo parenting. During their mutual commiseration, the dream of a first-class, cutting-edge clinic with an equally state-of-the-art day care for employees was created. Faster than Cody had imagined, he'd become Alex's partner and co-founder of the Maple Island Clinic off the coast of Massachusetts.

The day care had been a lifesaver, but Cody's problem this morning had been that children were supposed to show up already dressed for the day and in his five-year-old daughter's mind that included a properly tied hair-bow. Lizzy didn't consider herself dressed without a ribbon in her hair.

Like this morning, Cody sometimes worried he might not be enough for Jean and Lizzy. He often felt they needed that special attention that only a woman could provide. He shoved that thought away, his teeth clenching from the force of his resolve. He couldn't risk a repeat of the hell Rachael had put them through. What if he chose wrong again?

Enough of those thoughts. He didn't have time to review ugly memories. Besides being a single parent, as an orthopedic surgeon specializing in knees and legs, he had a busy clinic and a full surgery schedule this Monday morning to occupy his mind. Some attractive woman visiting a patient shouldn't even be a concern.

Heading down the hall, he soon entered his office and habitually checked the time. He could complete some paperwork and make a couple of phone calls before he was needed in the OR.

An hour later, dressed in green scrubs and matching surgical gown with mask in place, he pushed through the OR doors. He had a meniscus repair to perform. It always troubled him that he was intelligent enough to do such delicate surgery but he still hadn't been able to save Rachael.

His team was waiting for him. The patient was on the table with his left knee surrounded by blue sterile drapes.

Cody looked at Mark, the anesthesiologist.

"All set," Mark confirmed, without being asked.

"Everyone ready?" Cody glanced around the table.

All eyes focused on him then a feminine voice from across the patient said, "Yes."

His scrutiny fell on her. Dressed in the same surgical garb as he, all he could see of her was her enthralling green eyes. They were familiar but he didn't know why. "And you are?"

"Stacey Ryder, your new clinical nurse specialist. I thought I'd stand in today and see your technique. It makes it easier to sound confident in front of the family when I've seen the doctor in action."

Normally Cody would have met his replacement nurse before she started. Instead he had trusted the personnel department to handle it. His regular nurse would be out for a month, taking care of her aging mother after a surgery. He had just vetted this new one on paper, seeing she came with the highest recommendations. However, her straightforward approach hadn't been noted.

There were suppressed murmurs behind the masks of his team members. Were they as shocked by her boldness as he? As a rule, the people he worked with didn't use such an imperious tone with him.

Cody caught and held her attention. "You're welcome to stay but don't get in the way."

"Understood, Doctor."

Giving her a curt nod, he crisply announced, "Let's get this tennis player back on the court."

"Yes, sir," Stacey Ryder quipped with a note of humor in her voice as if she had given him a mental salute. He narrowed his eyes. She didn't blink.

Dismissing her, Cody looked at the knee, making sure it was the one he'd written his initials on. The patient's leg already had a tourniquet in place and was secured to the table in a padded leg holder. Cody made a small incision to prepare for the diagnostic camera that would give him a view of the joint. He located the damaged meniscus and probed it with a tiny metal hook.

"This is going to be a pretty extensive repair. I hope no one has early lunch plans. Shaver."

The surgical nurse handed the instrument to him. He trimmed the edges of the tear. "This isn't going to be enough."

"Why not?" his new clinical nurse asked.

"Because I'm not pleased with the blood flow."

She looked at him. "So, what're you going to do?"

He glared back at her. "Ms. Ryder, I don't usually teach procedure during my operations."

"I'm sure you don't but I'd like to know enough to help the families understand and also save you time when you talk to them."

Cody couldn't fault her logic. "I'm going to make the lining bleed and then suture it together. First I need to make another incision to work through to do that." As he did so, blood oozed into the field, making his visibility poor. Without him having to ask, Stacey used already prepared gauzes on forceps to wipe it away.

"We need to get that under control before I continue," he stated. "I'm ready to suture."

His surgical nurse handed him the equipment required.

"Nurse Ryder, I need you to keep the area clear while I work."

"Yes, sir." She replaced the gauze and dabbed the area.

Cody watched. "Good." He worked the thread into a neat stitch.

"Doctor, since you seem to have improved your tying skills since this morning, I'm going to speak to the family now. They must be anxious."

Cody frowned at her. Her eyes snapped with humor. That second he realized why he recognized those eyes. She was referring to his inability to tie Lizzy's bow. They would have a talk about her OR decorum later. His voice tight with disapproval, he said, "Please tell the family I'll be out to see them in soon."

"Yes, sir." She quietly left.

For some reason the room suddenly felt cooler.

Stacey was still sitting with the family when Dr. Brennan strolled into the waiting room with a smile on his face. She had to admit it was a nice one. For a while there, she hadn't been sure if he knew how to form one. It was so congenial she was sure if he turned it on her, her stomach would flutter. Stacey wrinkled her nose. Why would she think that?

Had she overstepped in the OR when she'd teased him about "tying" his stitches? By the steely look in his eye she might well have. Sometimes her humor was misplaced. She was so used to working in laid-back, often difficult conditions where levity was required. This wasn't one of those situations. In fact, this was the nicest, most upscale medical facility she'd ever been in.

When the director of the World Travel Nursing Agency had told her about her next assignment, she'd shared with Stacey information about the fabulous care given at the Maple Island Clinic. It turned out it was true, right down to the beautiful island and the top-notch physicians.

Dr. Brennan certainly knew his stuff. She'd seen enough good and bad surgeries on her journeys to recognize a surgeon with exceptional skills. Not just the abilities acquired through training and experience, but that special touch inherent in someone devoted to his patients' welfare. Did that quality extend to other areas of his life?

He'd been great with his daughter, despite his charming ineptness with her bow. It probably came more from being in a hurry rather than incompetence. Something about Dr. Brennan's manner made her believe he worked hard at being confident and competent in every aspect of his life. She also had the idea he was driven to keep any weakness or flaws well concealed.

"Here's Dr. Brennan now," Stacey said to the middle-aged mother of their patient seated beside her. Releasing her hand, Stacey stood. "I'm sure he can tell you more."

Dr. Brennan had pulled a long white lab coat over his scrubs. His thick chestnut hair was still mussed from removing his surgical cap. She guessed he'd only run a hand through it because a lock hung over his forehead. The effect gave him a less polished look than he'd had that morning in front of the day care. Deciding she liked this version better, Stacey stepped out of his way.

He sat on the edge of the chair she had vacated and turned to the mother. "Your son's doing very well and is in Recovery right now. He'll be in some pain, but I promise we're handling it. You'll be able to see him in about an hour."

"Oh, Dr. Brennan. Thank you for taking care of him. Do you think this'll get him back on the tennis court?"

He nodded. "I have complete confidence it will. Now, why don't you go get something to eat and meet him in his room?" He turned to Stacey. "Nurse, would you please direct his family to the room where Mr. Washington will be?"

Stacey wasn't sure where that would be, but she'd find out somehow. She wasn't about to make her ignorance of that detail obvious to him so she answered with confidence. "I'll be glad to."

His attention returned to Mrs. Washington and he

placed a hand on her shoulder. "If you need anything, will you let me or Nurse—"

"Please make it Stacey." She looked at the woman with warmth before giving Dr. Brennan a pointed stare.

A thin smile curved his lips and he nodded once before leaving the way he'd come.

Stacey settled the Washington family in the patient's room before returning to the waiting room to speak to the family of Dr. Brennan's next surgery patient. When she checked in with him during surgery he gave her a brief, concise pronouncement that the patient was doing as expected. She left with a "Thank you, Doctor." Again, she was with the family when he came in to speak to them.

Finished he stood, stepped away from the group and said, "Stacey, may I speak to you a moment?"

A shiver of uncertainty went through her. Yep, she'd overstepped. "Yes, sir."

In the hall, he slowed long enough to say, "I'll be doing rounds in thirty minutes. Meet me at my office in ten. Do you know where that is?"

"I'll find it."

He nodded. She was quickly learning it was his signature acknowledgment.

Stacey made sure she was a minute early when she knocked on his door.

"Come in."

His accent wasn't the typical clipped, sharp, New Englander one. What was his story? It didn't matter. She wouldn't be around long enough to really get to know him, or anyone else well. Four short weeks didn't leave much time to create friendships. That's how she'd spent most of her life. She never stayed in one place long enough to get close to people and start caring about them on a personal level, on purpose. She made sure to leave before she could be left. If you cared you got hurt. She'd had enough of that in her life.

Early in life after her father had left and then again when her mother had divorced her second husband, she'd learned not caring meant that you didn't feel pain. The ache had been so great when she'd been a child she never wanted it to happen again. She'd do anything to make that not occur, to the point of remaining distant. People disappointed her if she let them close enough. When her mother had brought home her third husband, Stacey hadn't even bothered to call him by his real name. Instead she made up a name for him, one she could easily forget. She'd spent most of her time in her room.

The only permanent person in her life was her mother and Stacey hadn't seen her in over a year. In fact, she was due for a visit that Stacey planned to make before she left for her next assignment in Ethiopia. As soon as this placement was done she would spend a couple of days with her mother then not bother again for another year. She couldn't rely on her mother, who had always had her own screwed-up life to worry about. The one time Stacey had let her guard down and let someone get too close romantically, he had disappointed her as well. Once again her heart had been crushed.

She'd been engaged. Had believed she had found the guy who would treat her as if she were special, one who would always be there for her, share the family with her that she'd never had. Instead she'd found out he'd been cheating on her. Their life together had been over before it had even properly started. Once again she was of no value to anyone. She'd ended their relationship with one of the same ugly scenes she'd witnessed her mother having when one of her relationships had ended.

That's when Stacey had decided seeing the world and devoting herself to professionally caring for people was safer than nurturing the terminally ill hope that someone would someday actually want her, see her as essential to their life. Now she didn't stay in one place long enough to allow a bond to form beyond what was necessary. It was better, simpler, and easier on her heart that way.

Dr. Brennan, sitting behind his desk, raised his dark head, his eyes studying her. She was sure his intent scrutiny wasn't missing a thing. That shrewdness must be part of the reason he was such a well-respected physician in his field. She had researched him on the internet before agreeing to the job.

"I want to apologize for my comment in the OR. That wasn't the place to tease you." She walked further into the room.

One of his brows rose slightly. "I'm not used to being teased, in or out of the OR."

Oops. She had no doubt that was true.

"We need to get to rounds. The girls have dance practice this evening."

Thankfully he'd changed the subject. "Girls? As in plural?"

Standing, he moved around the desk. "My daughters."

He was tall, her head only reached to his shoulder. His large open office seemed small with him in it. She'd only seen one child that morning. But he had another.

"Lizzy has an older sister, Jean. She's isn't quite so demanding and is far more independent. She'd already gone into day care when you came along." He twisted his lips. "And didn't require a bow."

Stacey grinned. There was affection in his voice when he spoke of his children. That alone made her admire him. She'd never heard that from a man while growing up. Mostly she'd just been in the way.

He led the way out the door.

Prone to chattering when she was nervous, Stacey said, "This is an amazing clinic. Nothing like what I've been working in while I was in South America."

"Thanks. It was a real answer to our prayers. Alex and I created a great place to work while still giving our children and the staff a quality place to stay while we do that." He stopped at a patient's door. "This is Mrs. Fitzpatrick. She had her surgery a week ago." Dr. Brennan was back in doctor mode as he knocked on the door.

At the sound of "Come in" they did, him leading the way.

A woman in her mid-sixties with vivid white hair cut in a fashionable style sat regally in a chair next to the windows. Across from her in a matching wingback was an older man, who complemented her appearance. They had the aura of wealth.

Stacey took a quick glance around the room. The bed alone said that the Maple Island Clinic was a cut above other medical facilities. It looked like a typical one that might be found in anybody's bedroom, but she was pretty sure that beneath the floral spread it functioned like a hospital bed. The view beyond the windows was of a spring-green grassy area leading to ocean waves. Stacey could well understand why people would want to come here to recuperate.

"Hello, Dr. Brennan," the woman said proudly. "I've been up and moving around today."

"That's good to hear." He stepped closer.

The older man stood and the two men shook hands.

Dr. Brennan turned toward her. "Mr. and Mrs. Fitzpatrick, this is my new nurse, Stacey Ryder."

Smiling at them, she said, "Please call me Stacey." Then she addressed the woman. "I understand you had a knee replacement."

"I did. Thanks to Dr. Brennan I'll finally be able to get on the floor with my grandkids."

Stacey's smile widened. Mrs. Fitzpatrick didn't seem the type to want to do that, but now she could. "That's great to hear."

"I'd like to check your incision, if I may?" Dr. Brennan asked.

Mrs. Fitzpatrick pulled her right pants leg up over her knee. Dr. Brennan went down on his heels to examine it closely. "It looks good. Now let me see you bend it."

The woman lifted it up and down. Stacey didn't miss how her lips tightened, but she didn't make a sound.

Dr. Brennan stood and put his hand on her shoulder. "I'm impressed. I can tell you've been working hard in physical therapy. I think you're about ready to go home."

Mrs. Fitzpatrick's smile was a bright one. "That's sooner than you had said."

"It pays to be a good patient," he responded, grinning.

Stacey enjoyed the moment. Dr. Brennan had a nice rapport with his patient. She hadn't seen much of that in her work in medical facilities in developing countries. There the patients came and left the same day. None of the doctors, and certainly none of the temporary nurses, had an opportunity to really get to know the patients. It was lovely to see that personal interaction in this clinic but at the same time it made her uncomfort-

able. She wasn't looking to become involved with anyone on any level.

Over the next few hours Stacey found out that Dr.
Brennan's bedside manner didn't just extend to the Fitz-
patricks. He treated all his patients with the same respect
and concern. Each time they saw someone new he took
the time to introduce Stacey, making her feel she was
part of his team, significant. That was an odd thought.

They were passing through the activity room where
the afternoon sun beamed in through the windows when
a weathered man sitting at a table lifted a hand in acknowledgment.

"Hey, Salty. Good to see you," Dr. Brennan greeted
him.

"Who's that with you?" Salty wanted to know.

"This is my new nurse. Stacey Ryder. Stacey, this is
Salty, our local hero."

Stacey couldn't miss the pink spreading across the
older man's cheeks, the wrinkles that gathered beside his
eyes and the straightening of his shoulders. "Aw, 'twas
nothing. Anyone would have done it." His gruff voice
was filled with pride.

"Done what?" she couldn't help but ask.

"We had a ferry accident a few months back. Salty
went out in his boat and helped save people."

"That sounds impressive." And she was impressed.

Salty shrugged his shoulders. "Glad I could help."

"We've got to be going. See you around." Dr. Brennan strolled on through the area.

"Nice to meet you." Stacey hurried to catch up with
the long-legged doctor.

They hadn't made it into the hall when Salty called,
"Hey, Doc, find a good woman and you've found a jewel."

Dr. Brennan raised a hand and kept walking. "Thanks. I'll remember that."

Stacey had seen the slight flinch of his shoulders before he'd waved off Salty's unsolicited advice. "What was that about?"

"Nothing. Salty is always dishing out his idea of wisdom."

Dr. Brennan didn't appear to think that particular piece of advice was very impressive. Were he and his wife having trouble? Whatever it was, it had nothing to do with her and so was none of her concern.

A few minutes later as they walked out of a patient's room a tall, sandy-blond man wearing a lab coat came toward them. "Hey, Cody. How's it going?"

"Well. Your staff has done wonders with Mrs. Fitzpatrick." Dr. Brennan passed her his hand computer on which he was making notes. "As uncooperative as she was before surgery, I'm impressed by how far she's come in such a short time."

"What can I say? We're good!" The man chuckled, then gave her a questioning look. "Hi, I'm Alex Kirkland, your medical director."

"I'm Stacey Ryder, Dr. Brennan's temporary nurse."

"That's right, Marsha's out taking care of her mother. Welcome. We're glad to have you," Dr. Kirkland said. "Feel free to call me Alex."

She liked him. He wasn't quite as stuffy as Dr. Brennan. "Alex. I'm glad to be here. Didn't I read somewhere that it was you and Dr. Brennan who started this clinic?"

"Yeah, that was us." Pride filled his voice.

An attractive woman with a riot of red hair headed their way with a bounce in her step. She called, "Hey, Alex, you have a minute?"

Alex's eyes lit up before he turned. "I always do for you."

"Aw, you do care." She joined them.

Stacey suspected there was a deeper meaning to their greeting by the way Alex lightly touched her elbow to direct her attention to Stacey.

"Maggie, this is Stacey Ryder, Cody's clinical nurse for the next few weeks."

Maggie extended her hand. "Maggie Green, one of the physiotherapists around here. I specialize in hydro and equine therapy. Glad to have you. I hope you enjoy your stay." She turned to Alex. "I hate to drag you away but I need to talk to you about one of the twins for a sec."

Alex shrugged. "Duty calls. Good to have you, Stacey. Don't let Cody overwork you while you're here." He followed Maggie down the hall toward the hydro area.

Stacey looked at Cody "She seems like fun."

"That's not what Alex thought for a while. Now he'd agree with you."

They continued down the hall.

Uncharacteristic curiosity had gotten the better of her and Stacey had researched the founding of the clinic. After meeting a few people, she'd already figured out the internet didn't tell the entire story of Maple Island Clinic. Doing the research in person with one of the founders, especially a particularly handsome one, was an invitation to get personal. Taking a breath for courage, Stacey asked, "So how did you and Alex decide you wanted to start this facility? By your accents you don't come from the same part of the country."

He looked at her for a moment as if he was deciding whether or not to answer. "We don't. We met at a conference. Single guys with childcare issues in common.

Next thing I knew we were coming up with this clinic idea." He turned the corner and started down another hall. "I'm originally from California."

"That makes sense. One coast for another." That seemed a pretty dramatic move for a specialty surgeon of Brennan's caliber. Was there more to it than a chance meeting at a conference? Had something else pushed him into the move? She shouldn't pry further yet she couldn't stop herself. "Was that a hard sell to your family?"

"No. The girls were so small they were good with it."

"Your wife?" Stacey winced silently. She had already asked too many questions.

"She was already out of the picture." His words were flat and final.

Stacey let go a private sigh of relief. He'd closed the door on that subject, slammed it shut.

They walked back to his office in silence. There he said, "I'll see you in surgery at six in the morning." Then he literally closed the door in her face.

So much for Mr. Charming.

CHAPTER TWO

Two days later Cody picked up the girls from dance practice. It wasn't his favorite night of the week because it was always so busy. To make it less stressful he usually took them out to dinner. Tonight they were going to Brady's Bistro and Bakery for pizza. They all loved the thin slices and best of all he didn't have to cook.

As often as possible he tried to give the girls nutritious meals. He was trying to make up for the time when they hadn't had them. By the end of his marriage, Rachael hadn't cared enough to prepare meals. Every cent she'd been able to get her hands on had gone toward her next fix.

Cody had promised himself that his girls would have home-cooked, locally grown, wholesome food as much as possible. For the most part he'd managed to achieve that. Still, it was nice to get out of the kitchen and concentrate on having more quality time with his kids.

He held the door to the bistro open. The place was full, noisy with the sounds of talking, laughter and dishes rattling. He looked around the space with its red chrome tabletops and yellow chairs covered in plastic. The black and white tile floors added to the fifties vibe.

With a moan and a hunger pang, he resigned himself to

the fact they would have to wait. He scanned the dining area with irritation. It wouldn't be a short wait. Stepping to the left a pace, he searched again. There was a booth with some empty seats. Looking closer, he saw Stacey sitting in one corner of it.

The thought that it wasn't a good idea to join her was interrupted by Jean's plaintive announcement, "I'm hungry."

Cody drew a fortifying breath for reasons he couldn't put a finger on. They had worked well together over the last few days. Stacey had a great rapport with the patients, could anticipate many of the things he needed done, and she took direction without complaint. Most of all she was friendly and always wore a smile. So why did he have an issue with her? Could it be he found her attractive and that made him uncomfortable? Even if that was the cause of his hesitation, he had an immediate problem to solve that overrode his feelings.

"This way, girls." He weaved between the tables, glancing back to make sure they were following.

When he reached Stacey's table she looked up in surprise. "Dr. Brennan."

"Hey, do you mind if we join you? There don't seem to be any more seats and the girls are *very* hungry."

"Please do." She waved her hand toward the open places and smiled at the girls.

"Daddy, do you know her?" Jean asked in a suspicious tone.

Lizzy gave Stacey a look of wonder. Finally, she burst out with, "You're the woman who fixed my bow."

Stacey smiled. "Yes, I am. You're Lizzy, right?"

His younger daughter bobbed her head up and down.

"Yes, I know her," he said to Jean, then looked at Stacey. "And this is Jean." He placed a hand on his other daughter's shoulder.

Jean gave Stacey the sulky look that had become her standard greeting to unknown women. His elder daughter was having the most difficulty with the loss of her mother. She could remember Rachael being a part of their lives, but had been too young to understand her mother's problems.

"Hey," Jean said belatedly, with zero enthusiasm.

"Hi, Jean. It's nice to meet you." Stacey gave her an encouraging smile. "I work with Dr. Brennan...uh...your father. Why don't you sit over here beside me?" She patted the bench beside her.

Jean offered her father a doubtful look. He nodded and gave her a light nudge of encouragement. Jean slid in beside Stacey. He said to her, "And you can call me Cody."

Stacey instantly produced the smile that made him want to return one. "Cody it is."

He appreciated the way she pronounced his name, as if it were a sweet she was tasting for the first time and finding she liked it.

"You go first," Lizzy said, leaving Cody no choice but to scoot in until he faced Stacey. His knees bumped hers. Their looks caught. "Sorry."

"No problem."

His fascination with Stacey's green eyes was broken when Lizzy scrambled into her spot beside him.

The awkwardness he was experiencing disappeared when Brigid Brady, their waitress today, walked up to the table. "Hi, Jean and Lizzy. Cody."

Her look lingered on him a little longer than mere politeness allowed, much to his annoyance. More than once she'd made unmistakable overtures. He wasn't interested in a relationship with her now or even later. He glanced at Stacey. She watched them with a quizzical smile. No, she definitely hadn't missed Brigid's extra attention.

"Uh... Brigid, we'd like a medium pepperoni and cheese pizza." His gaze returned to Stacey. "I'm sorry. Have you already ordered?"

"No. But pizza sounds good."

"Then make that a large," he said to Brigid. "And four sodas." He looked at Stacey again.

"That work for you?"

"It does."

"It'll be out in a few minutes," Brigid said with a huff of disgust in her voice.

As she left a soft chuckle came from across the table. "Charming in and out of the OR, I see."

He twisted the corner of his mouth and shrugged.

Her attention went to Jean. "I heard you're a dancer."

"I take dancing. I'm not very good, though." Jean stared at the tabletop.

"I take it too," Lizzy proudly announced.

Stacey acknowledged her with a look of wide-eyed wonderment and asked, "You're a dancer too? Awesome!"

Stacey's focus was completely on his girls and it was genuine. They needed that in their lives. Their mother had never been there for them. The few women he'd had anything to do with in the years since his divorce had been more one-night stands than anything. He certainly had not brought them home to meet his daughters.

"That's great. I never had a chance to learn." Stacey leaned toward them as if enthralled with what Jean and Lizzy were telling her.

"Why not?" Lizzy asked, but Jean appeared uninterested.

"I moved around a lot and my mother didn't put me in any classes."

"You could come to ours," Lizzy offered so emphatically that Cody couldn't help but chuckle. The action felt good. He could only imagine Stacey in an eight and under class of girls in tutus.

"I think that would be fun but I don't think I'll be on Maple Island long enough to take lessons now either." Stacey hadn't taken her eyes off the girls, especially Jean.

"Where're you going?" Jean asked, frowning at the tabletop.

"In a few weeks I'll be going to Ethiopia after a quick stop to visit my mother for a couple of days."

Jean sat straighter in her chair. "Ethiopia. We've been studying about that country in geography. It's in Africa, isn't it? That's a long way away."

For once his oldest was engaged in the conversation. Stacey had a carefree manner about her. That unique congeniality came from living life on the move with the ease of the wind. Her life was a complete contrast to his. Still, he liked her ability to interact with people as if she'd known them forever. He'd seen her use that skill with his patients and now with his girls. She never treated people as though they were strangers. That was a talent to admire.

"It is, but I'm looking forward to going," Stacey said.

"Why?" Lizzy asked.

"Because I'll get to help lots of boys and girls."

"How?" Jean wanted to know, finally turning to study Stacey's face.

"I'm a nurse. So I'll help them feel better."

Jean lowered her gaze again but stopped short of the

table surface. With a tentative touch, she fingered the wooden bead bracelet on Stacey's wrist.

"You like it? It's from Bolivia."

"Boo-liver-a," Lizzy said.

He and Stacey tried not to laugh.

"Bo-li-via," Stacey said slowly. "It's in South America." She turned back to Jean. "A girl about your age made it for me." She took it off and handed it to Jean. "You can have it. I bet she'd like to know that a girl in America is wearing it."

Jean looked at her father in silent question. He nodded. "If Stacey says it's okay."

"It is. I don't get to wear it enough. If you have it, Jean, I'll know it'll be cared for."

"Thank you." Jean's words were almost inaudible as she placed the bracelet on her slim wrist.

Stacey continued patiently engaging his girls in conversation until the drinks and pizza arrived.

"I hope you didn't feel forced into eating this just because it was what we were having." Cody put a slice on each of the girl's plates.

"Not at all. I don't always get pizza in the places I go." Stacey gave Jean and Lizzy a conspiratorial look. "I have to fill up when I have a chance." They nodded in simultaneous agreement.

Cody asked the girls what they'd done today, particularly how school had gone.

"I thought you stayed in the day care," Stacey said.

"We do," both replied at the same time.

"They go there before school opens, and then are transported to school and back again when school finishes." Cody took a bite of his pizza.

"Nice and convenient." Stacey pulled a second slice

from the pizza sheet. Cheese strung out, breaking as she turned its triangle edge into her mouth.

Cody held his breath as the cheese landed on her chin. "That was the plan when Alex and I came up with the idea. So far it has worked out great."

"You have cheese on your chin," Jean pointed out.

"I do?" Stacey wiped her napkin across her cheek.

Lizzy yelped. "It's still there."

Stacey dabbed the napkin over her face again.

"You didn't get it." Lizzy giggled.

"Here, let me help." Cody reached across the table with his napkin in hand. As he removed the cheese, his gaze rose to find Stacey watching him. Her eyes were a forest green, and there was a twinkle in them. They looked like an inviting place where he could go and forget his cares.

"Hey, Daddy. Can we go get an ice cream?" Jean asked, dropping a crust on her plate.

Jerked back to reality, Cody quickly returned his hand to his side of the table. "Yeah, sure," he said before he'd thought about it.

"Yay," both girls yelled.

He put a finger to his mouth. "Shush. Not so loud. We're inside."

"You want to go with us?" Jean asked as she and Lizzy turned to Stacey.

She looked at him briefly. He did his best not to react one way or another but he didn't think that was a good idea. For him or the girls.

Finally, Stacey said, "I don't believe so this time. I've had too much pizza. Maybe next time."

To his amazement, Jean looked as disappointed as he felt. Why? he questioned himself on both accounts. Stacey had managed to forge some kind of relationship with his elder daughter who normally didn't warm up to strangers, especially female ones. So, what was it about Stacey that had him and Jean doing and saying things they didn't ordinarily do?

He paid for their meal despite Stacey arguing that she needed to cover her share. "Because of you we didn't have to wait to eat. The least I can do is get your meal."

"Thank you, then."

They were exiting the bistro when Jean pointed out the poster about the island's Founder's Day Weekend taped to the glass window. "Daddy, Fleur has been teaching us dances at day care. She wants us to do them on Saturday of Founder's Day Weekend. We have to have costumes."

"Costumes. That sounds like fun. I love to dress up," Stacey commented as she held the door open for the girls to exit.

Cody almost groaned out loud. Putting together costumes was his least favorite thing to do. Imagination wasn't his strong suit. They'd had to have outfits for the library's Fright Night a couple of months back. They had gone as trolls only because those had been the only costumes he could find in the store. He believed he should at least be allowed a full year before he had to come up with more. The side of his brain he used most held facts and numbers. He had to stretch to the other to be creative *and* inventive. Hopefully, Fleur, a recent patient and now the soon-to-be wife of Rick Fleming, a doctor at the clinic, would provide some guidelines or ideas.

They were out on the sidewalk when Stacey asked, "Founder's Day Weekend. What's that?"

"It's so much fun," Lizzy said, hopping with anticipation. "I like the pony rides."

Cody rubbed the top of his younger daughter's head

and chuckled. "You like anything that has to do with a pony." He regarded Stacey. "We celebrate the settling of the island. The story goes that after a long and very hard winter a few early settlers traveled from the mainland over to the island, seeking food. They found the maple trees and tapped them. The maple syrup helped restore the strength of the people. No one really knows whether it is true or not, but we remember those early settlers and focus on maple syrup by having a Founder's Day Weekend. With all the trimmings—food, entertainment and fireworks. Everyone turns out for the event."

"I've never been to a Founder's Day anywhere," Stacey said.

"You'll come see us dance?" Lizzy stopped twisting to and fro long enough to ask.

"Of course I will." Stacey assured her. "If I am still here."

Jean and Lizzy grinned from ear to ear.

"Well, we'd better be going. Thanks again for sharing your table with us." He was uneasy on some level with what was happening between Stacey and his girls, as well as his reaction to her. The whole meal had seemed far too family-like for his comfort.

"No problem. I'll see you in the morning. Bye, Jean and Lizzy." Stacey glanced back at him as she turned. "Thanks again for the pizza."

He nodded. She lifted a hand and strolled away, looking in shop windows as she went. Why did he feel some of the pleasure in the evening was walking away from them?

Two days later, Stacey fixed a cup of hot chocolate in the employees' kitchen and pulled on her sweater. She loved the ocean and didn't always get an assignment near one, so she planned to take her afternoon break on the sundeck.

She eased into a chair. Being early April, the days were still cool. Raising her face to the sun, she closed her eyes. She'd been at the clinic for almost a week already. To her surprise she'd relished every minute of it. After living in little more than huts most of her professional life, she enjoyed staying in the tiny cottage called Paradise, facing the harbor. It was a slice of heaven. The village was pretty and she was slowly working her way through all the eating places. People were friendly and she was at ease here. She would miss it when she left.

Inhaling the damp salt air deeply, she released it slowly. The seagulls squawked nearby as the waves rolled in. Oh, yes, this was a great place to recharge her batteries. She needed this downtime in her life. This would be her first weekend on the island and she planned to do more of this.

A hand touched her arm. Her eyes jerked open. Cody's dark coffee gaze looked down at her. Determination, along with a touch of something else, etched his features.

"I've been searching everywhere for you. I need you to come with me."

She'd been so absorbed in her thoughts she'd not heard either him approaching or apparently her phone ringing.

"Where're we going?" She thought through the fog of surprise and tried not to react to his touch, which had left her forearm tingling, tiny hairs raised by goosebumps. Her reaction to him had to stop. She was too old for a crush.

"Boston. We have an emergency. I need you at the helipad in ten." He was already walking away.

Stacey rushed into the clinic behind him. She spoke to his back when she asked, "Do I need to prepare a bag, take anything?"

"They'll have everything we need there. I'll see you at the pad. I have to check on the girls."

She was waiting at the helicopter pad when Cody arrived. His lips were moving rapidly as he spoke into his phone. A furrow creased his forehead. The blades of the machine were already humming as they climbed aboard. She was a nervous flier. She gulped and climbed aboard. A high level of trepidation zipped through her.

She fumbled with her seatbelt. Cody reached over and clipped it into place. She gave him a weak smile. "Thanks."

He cupped his ear, shook his head and mouthed, "Use headphones," then pointed to them hanging above her.

Stacey placed them on her head.

"This the first time you've ever been in a helicopter?" He spoke through the headpiece.

She looked at him and nodded. Over the years she'd ridden in jeeps and in the back of trucks over rutted, washed-out roads, and once in a small plane, which she hadn't liked any better than the helicopter. Apparently, her fear was showing.

"There's a button on your headphones just above your right ear. Push it when you talk and release it so you can hear me."

She found the button and did as he instructed. "You can hear me now?"

"I can."

The helicopter shifted, and the wind swooshed before the machine started to lift. Her hands gripped the edge of the seat as she stared out the front windshield. Seconds later her right hand was prised off the seat. Cody took it in his, holding it. His hand was large, enveloping hers and radiating a promise that he was there for her. Unsure what was more disconcerting, Cody holding her hand or the flight, she gripped his fingers tightly like the lifeline they were.

She dared to glance at him. His eyes were intently focused forward. Was he already envisioning the surgery ahead of him? She'd gotten to know many of his facial expressions over the last few days. More than once she had seen those worry lines on his brow, the twinkle in his eyes when he talked about his girls and the rare but always breathtaking event when he laughed. Which happened usually when he was talking to Alex.

She relaxed somewhat and Cody released her hand. Her growing security was gone. Placing fisted hands in her lap, she looked out the side window. The view of the island was amazing. It was green, a luscious ornament in the middle of a vibrant blue dotted with tiny spots of white.

As they sped out over the water she peeked at Cody again. He looked much as he had earlier. It was as if he were somewhere else. Her attention moved to the approaching coastline. The tall ship moored in Boston harbor was clearly visible along with a few of the historical buildings. They flew by them and over the modern structures. Suddenly the helicopter went into hover mode.

Panic tightened her chest. As she reached for the edge of her seat Cody took hold of her hand once more. Gratefully she clung to it.

There was a crackle in her headset before his voice fill her ears. "The take-off and landing are always the worst."

She gave him what she hoped was a look of gratitude, but she worried that her actual expression appeared pained. Not soon enough for her, the helicopter settled on the top of what she assumed was the hospital. Too soon Cody let go of her hand. With his simple action he had shown more awareness of her needs than her mother or fiancé ever had.

He climbed out of the helicopter and stopped long enough to help her down. After they were out from under the blades, he was on the phone. His questions were clipped and his responses short.

Soon they were on the elevator, going down.

Cody leaned against the opposite wall from her as they rode. "Our case is a seventeen-year-old boy involved in a car accident. His knee has been crushed and both his tibia and fibula are broken. When the general surgeon is done with some internal injuries I'll get to work. To add to the trickiness of the surgery, the boy is the son of a state senator. I understand the kid was running from the police when the accident happened so make sure you don't speak out of turn to anyone. The family should be in a private waiting room. I'll talk to them before I go into the OR."

"I understand." She had no experience dealing with high-profile cases, but she had no intention of disappointing Cody.

She hurried to keep up as he took long strides toward the surgery department. She waited to the side while he quietly conferred with another doctor. Done, Cody stepped to the hallway door. He said to her, "This way."

They walked down the hall side by side. Soon they came to a closed door. He opened it and she followed him through. Inside was a room with cushioned chairs that didn't match. She was sure they had been pulled from various places. People in suits sat and stood, all talking on phones.

"Mr. and Mrs. Clark?" Cody said, loud enough so he could be heard over the din.

"I'm Mr. Clark." A man with graying temples stepped toward them. "This is my wife. Senator Ann Clark."

A woman with a stately bearing and bloodshot eyes rose from the chair in the corner.

Cody stepped forward and offered his hand. "Senator Clark, I'm Dr. Cody Brennan. I'll be taking care of your son's knee and leg."

She nodded. "I understand you're the best at this type of surgery."

"I'll certainly be doing my best for your son."

"His name is James." The senator leaned against her husband.

"This is Stacey Ryder, my clinical nurse. She'll be keeping you updated on how things are going in surgery. If you have any questions or concerns you let her know."

Stacey nodded and gave the parents a professional smile of reassurance.

"How long should James be in there?" The senator sniffled. "It's already been hours."

Cody's grave look didn't waver. "My guess is it'll be after midnight before you can see James. Now I have to go. I'll be out to speak to you as soon as I'm done in the OR."

The terrified parents just stared at him hopefully.

Cody lifted his chin toward the door. Stacey followed him out.

"I'll show you the OR I'm using. Sit with them for a few minutes then come check in with me. I want to give them as much reassurance as possible. Based on what

I've been told over the phone, the surgery is going to be a tough one."

They entered the surgical unit. Cody was greeted by a couple of people in surgical scrubs. At the OR unit desk he introduced her to the clerk. While they were there a man hurried up to them. Again, Cody introduced her. It was nice he remembered to do so because it would have been easy for him to get caught up in the case and forget she was there. It made her feel valued. The man was the surgeon's assistant who would be aiding Cody.

The two men went into a deep discussion about the amount of damage to the boy's leg.

Cody finished with, "Then we'll plan to stabilize everything tonight and go in again in a day or two to complete the repair. The swelling needs to go down and James needs to be stable first."

"The general surgeon should be through in about fifteen minutes. They'll be ready for you then." His surgical assistant was already headed down the hall.

"Sounds good. That'll give me time for something to drink and a granola bar."

The striding assistant called over his shoulder, "The dinner of champions."

Cody looked at her. "Come join me?"

Stacey followed him to a small break room a few doors down containing a couple of vending machines.

"May I offer you dinner?" Cody waved his hand toward the machines. She couldn't help but smile at his levity. "I suggest you have something. It'll be a long night." He pulled some bills out of his pocket and looked at them.

Stacey had left the island without even thinking about getting her purse. She was at his mercy in more ways than one. "My, Doctor, you do know how to turn a girl's head with a meal." She tried for her best nineteen-forties seductive-movie-star voice.

He looked over his shoulder and gave her a dry smile. "I'll try to do better in the future."

"In that case, for now I'll have a protein bar and a bottle of water, please."

Cody nodded. "Good choice. I'll have the same." He fed money into the slot.

With their food in hand, they sat at a small table with only two chairs.

"Are you sure this meager fare will be enough to get you through surgery?" She didn't hide her concern. When had she taken on worrying about him? Surely it was just one human being feeling concern about another and not something more.

Chewing, he studied her a moment. "I've gone on far less."

"I'm sure that isn't healthy."

"Maybe not, but necessary sometimes." He took a long draw on his water. She watched his throat as it went down. A day's worth of beard growth gave him a sexy edgy look. A little less buttoned up and more uninhibited. She liked it. He needed to let go somewhat.

"Is something wrong?" He stared her back to reality.

"Uh...nothing. Just thinking." To her dismay, her cheeks grew warm.

"About what?" Cody watched her much too closely.

Yeah, like she would admit she'd been thinking about how sexy he was. Her eyes didn't meet his as she spoke. "I was just wondering about who's watching the girls." *That was such a lie.*

Cody gave her a suspicious look as if he suspected she hadn't spoken the truth. "When Alex and I set up the clinic we knew we would have to occasionally be away for emergencies, so we set up an after-hours plan through the day care. Someone who works there is always on call. That person will come to my home and make sure the girls are taken care of. Even see they get to school. Because the girls are familiar with the person, they don't usually mind."

Stacey pursed her lips in thought, seriously impressed with such planning. "Nice thinking. Maple Island Clinic is really special."

"Thanks. We tried to think of everything." He shrugged. "If we didn't, we've figured it out as we've gone along." Cody stood. "I've got to head to surgery."

She needed to check in with James's parents.

"Just ask the unit clerk for anything you need. Give me half an hour to assess what I'll have to do, then you can come and get a report."

"Will do."

He gave her a wry smile and went out the door.

Cody was in the process of resecting the damaged skin when one of the surgical nurses said, "Doctor, I'm not feeling well." She ran for the door.

"Get some help in here!" He already had his hands full with the mangled leg and now he was short a nurse.

Another nurse in the room said, "At this time of night we'll have to call someone in."

"I need those hands now." The case was tough enough without this issue.

The ill nurse hadn't been gone a minute when the phone rang. No one could stop long enough to answer it. A few minutes later, with a mask over her mouth, Stacey stuck her head in the door.

"Dr. Brennan—"

"Scrub in. I need you in here," he barked, not even taking the time to look at her.

The door closed and a short time later Stacey entered. "Where do you want me?"

"Stand beside me. I need you to resect and clean the blood away so I can see." He had no more time to give directions. If any more tissue was lost then the boy would require skin grafts.

"Little to the left, Stacey. That's right."

As they worked he noted that he had to give her fewer instructions. Stacey anticipated his next move. "All right, let's get these bone splinters out of here."

His surgical nurse held a metal bowl as he picked bone pieces from the muscle.

"That looks like all of it." Now he could start trying to repair the jumbled mess.

"Doctor, I think I saw one more." Stacey pointed to a spot and dabbed it with gauze.

"Where?" He searched the area. "Ah, got it. Nice catch, Stacey."

She cleared the area again while he used the tweezers to remove the sliver before blood covered it again. "Excellent. Now, let's get this boy's leg pieced together."

Everyone worked patiently and efficiently over the next few hours arranging veins, ligaments and putting screws into bones as they put the human puzzle back together.

It was almost morning when he, Stacey and the other staff walked out of the OR. Cody pulled his surgical gown and hat off, dropping them into the cloth bin beside the door. He was acquainted with tough surgery but this one had definitely been in the top three he'd ever done.

The boy had damaged his leg almost to the point of no return. He would have additional surgeries ahead of him, painful rehabilitation and a limp.

"Job well done, all." He turned to Stacey. "Nice work in there. How much surgical training have you had?"

"Very little."

She sounded exhausted but there had been no complaints from her. She'd done what needed doing without question. He couldn't have been prouder of the work they'd accomplished.

Stacey stripped off her surgical clothes in record time and was headed out the door. "I need to speak to the parents. They must be crazy with worry since I just disappeared on them."

Cody hadn't thought of that. "Please tell them I'll be right out."

Hours later he and Stacey were standing at the ferry port, watching the vessel dock.

"I'm sorry the helicopter couldn't come get us. It's out, bringing one of Rafael's patients in." Cody watched the water froth as the ferry, its massive engines rumbling, eased beside the dock.

Stacey shrugged. "Part of the price of living on an island is living by the ferry schedule. It's better than swimming."

Cody chortled deep in his chest. "That I can agree with. Especially since the water isn't all that warm here. And it's too early and too far for a morning swim."

"I like the beach but I'm too darned tired to enjoy it today. All I want is my bed." She stepped onto the ferry.

"I couldn't agree more." He was by her side once more. "You were good in the OR and with the senator as well.

What's a nurse with those skills doing traipsing around the world?" As a general rule he didn't ask women personal questions, but for some reason he wanted to know more about this one, who was such an enigma. The need to learn what made her tick was beyond his control.

"Much the same thing as here, nursing."

Something in her tone, or lack of it, made him believe there was more to it than that. "But why the traveling part?"

Her slight frown suggested she was reluctant to answer yet she lifted a shoulder nonchalantly. "With a mother who has been married three times and is currently working on her fourth, I never really lived in one place very long. Being a traveling nurse was just an extension of that. It also gives me a chance to do all types of nursing in innumerable types of circumstances."

She was about going from one place to another, whereas he was about staying put. He wanted stability and calm in his life. He already knew what it was like to live daily with the anxiety of uncertainty. He pressed his lips together. Was Stacey's reluctance to settle down generated by fear as well?

They made their way inside to one of the bench seats. The engines rumbled as the ferry pulled away from the port. The sky was an orange pink over Maple Island, making it appear on fire. The best thing he'd ever done had been to move to the island. "So on-the-job training gave you those surgical skills."

She yawned behind the back of her hand. "Yes, even in developing countries a general practitioner will do major surgery if it's in the right place at the right time." She gave him a pensive look. "I know the clinic is great and all, but to move all the way from California seems a little extreme."

She'd deliberately changed the subject. Did she not want to talk about herself? He sure didn't. "Yeah, but it was a necessary one."

"How's that?"

Now he was the one hesitant to answer. But she'd responded to his difficult question so it was only fair that he do the same. "I'd gone through an ugly divorce and the girls and I needed to start over. Have a change." He leaned back, trying to get as comfortable as possible on the hard bench.

"Their mother didn't care that you took them so far away?" She watched him with disconcerting intensity.

He shrugged, trying to appear as uncaring as possible. "It didn't matter. She's no longer in their lives."

Stacey covered another yawn. "I see."

Cody doubted that she did, but he wasn't going into it any further.

"I don't want to be rude but I've got to close my eyes for a few minutes."

He stretched his legs out and crossed them at the ankles. "Not rude at all. It was a long night."

The ferry gently rocked. In minutes Stacey's breathing turned even. When her head tipped forward Cody put his arm around her shoulder and brought her to him. Her head rested on his chest. It had been a long time since he'd held a sleeping woman. Unable to resist, he brushed his cheek against her hair. It was as soft as it looked and smelled faintly of the peaches he remembered.

She murmured, shifted toward him then settled.

Cody closed his eyes. It seemed only seconds later the push of hands on his chest woke him.

Stacey's eyes were wide and her hair wild as she stared at him in alarm. She had such expressive eyes. Cody couldn't imagine her telling a convincing lie.

"I'm sorry I went to sleep on you. I hope I didn't drool on you." She brushed at his chest, the tips of her fingers leaving hot spots through the fabric of his shirt.

He grinned. "I didn't mind. Your head was bobbing, and I felt sorry for you. Especially after I'd already woke you once today…uh…yesterday. I didn't want to do it again."

"I wasn't asleep on the deck. I was thinking. Enjoying the sunshine." She stretched, showing a hint of skin at her waist before she tugged at her clothes, adjusting them.

His body reacted in ways that had been dormant for far too long. This was his nurse. He had no business ogling her. He couldn't help himself, though. Something about Stacey made his blood warm. He grinned. "Looked like sleeping on the job to me."

She stood over him, her hands on her hips. "I do not sleep on the job. Ever."

He winked at her. Even after a long night Stacey looked amazing. She had a knack for making him smile. There was a brightness to her that somehow made life look sunnier. He wanted to capture that. Hold it close. He reached for her but stopped himself, letting his hand fall to his thigh. "I was just kidding."

Kidding. He wasn't a kidder. What was she doing to him?

CHAPTER THREE

STACEY CONTINUED DOWN the path leading to the harbor.
The day was beautiful. The sun shone brightly, seagulls
swooped and squawked. Sailboats and small fishing craft
bobbed in the sparkling water. Had she found paradise?

She'd slept well past noon the day before, exhausted
from her all-nighter with Cody. To her horror she had
actually fallen asleep on him. Yet she had to admit it
had been nice to wake up in a man's strong arms. Especially his.

Cody was far better natured, more tender-hearted,
than she'd assumed, given her initial assessment of his
character. Just thinking about being so close to him raised
goose-bumps on her arms. She liked him too much. What
would it be like to have a few weeks of fun with him?

No, she couldn't act on that idea, even if he wanted
to. Cody and his daughters didn't need someone flitting
into their personal lives, disrupting them and then leaving. More than that, he was her boss. Mixing business
and pleasure often didn't turn out well.

He didn't strike her as a fling kind of guy. He had
two little girls he adored, and was incredibly protective
of them. All Stacey knew about relationships was that
when the going got difficult then people left and never

looked back. Even her ex-fiancé had followed that phi-
losophy. At least she'd found out about his affair before
they had married. Now she did all the leaving. She didn't
wait around for it to happen to her.

Long ago Stacey had concluded it was easier not to
even attempt marriage and parenthood. Stay loose and
laid-back. Enjoy what came, but not get too involved.
She was happier that way. While everything about Cody
screamed commitment. That alone should make her keep
her distance. She needed to focus on enjoying her time
on Maple Island and not go anywhere near Cody Brennan outside the clinic.

From the harbor she made her way into town. Though
she'd only been on the island for a week, she could tell the
population was increasing. The tourist crowd had started
creeping in as the spring weather warmed up quickly. She
took a seat on an empty bench in front of the library so
she could people-watch for a few minutes.

She looked across the street to see Lizzy coming her
way with her hair pulled back at the nape of her neck.
The child wore a sweatshirt, jeans and sneakers.

"Hey, Stacey," the little girl called out.

So much for staying out of Cody's life outside the
clinic. "Well, hey, there."

Lizzy plopped down. "What you doing?"

Stacey searched the area. "Does your father know
where you are?" Surely she wasn't by herself. It wouldn't
be like Cody to let Lizzy run around the island unsu-
pervised. He was a better parent than Stacey's had ever
been. She spied Cody and Jean coming out of a store.
Her heart skipped a beat.

Cody's dark looks and air of authority made him a
fine-looking man. Dressed in a button-down plaid shirt

with a navy zippered fleece vest over it and jeans, he couldn't have been more island casual or handsome. Tall, with those broad shoulders she knew well, he drew responses from all the women passing him. He captivated her for sure. Somehow she needed to get beyond this infatuation with him.

She regarded the charming cherub next to her. "I was just out for a walk."

"Hey, Daddy. I'm over here." Lizzy waved.

His tight look of worry eased into one of relief. He started across the cobbled street in their direction with Jean beside him. As soon as he was within hearing distance he spoke sharply to Lizzy. "I told you to wait outside the store."

"I saw Stacey and I wanted to say hello." Lizzy seemed to miss how concerned her father was.

Cody stepped closer and leaned down, gaining the girl's attention. "Next time you ask me before you go somewhere. I need to know where you are."

"Yes, Daddy," she said meekly.

Stacey tried to lighten the mood. She smiled. "Hey, Jean, Cody."

"Hi." Cody stepped back and looked at her. His voice hadn't lightened much.

Jean just watched her, not saying anything but obviously curious.

"Well, we need to be going." Cody looked at Lizzy and offered his hand. "Enjoy your day, Stacey."

Lizzy took hold of it and jumped to his side. She smiled at Stacey. "We're going to catch lobster and eat it and build a fire on the beach."

"That sounds like fun." And it did.

"It is, so much fun. The best." Lizzy almost hummed with excitement.

"Come on, let's not bother Stacey anymore." Cody tugged on Lizzy's hand.

"Daddy, can Stacey come lobster hunting with us?" Lizzy craned her neck to see her father's face.

Cody looked unsure as his eyes cut to Stacey. "Lizzy, I don't think Stacey—"

Lizzy yanked on his hand. "Daddy, we can show her how to set the trap, and row the boat, everything."

Getting more involved with Cody and his girls was the last thing Stacey planned to do. "Thanks for asking but I really should go home." She stood, intending to step away.

"Don't you want to catch lobster with us?" Lizzy asked, giving Stacey a serious frown.

"It's so much fun." She turned to Cody. "Tell her, Daddy."

It took a moment before he asked, "Have you ever put out a lobster pot?"

Stacey considered him, then Jean, then Lizzy. "No."

He placed his hand on Jean's shoulder. "Everyone should have the experience at least once."

"You need to come." Jean offered her first words since she and Cody had walked up. "It's my favorite thing to do too." Lizzy grinned at her. Cody's gaze met Stacey's. She watched his chest expand then he released a breath as if he had made a huge decision. "You should definitely join us."

Going with them wasn't a wise move, but it would only be for an evening and it wouldn't be just Cody and her—his daughters would be with them. Against her better judgment and because she couldn't resist their urging she said, "Okay."

Decision made, she planned to enjoy herself.

She joined Cody and the girls on their walk to his house. It turned out that he lived in a home not very far from Paradise Cottage. It was built in the saltbox style that was so common in that area. Yellow with a red door, it implied everyone was welcome. She loved it immediately.

The girls entered ahead of Cody and her, leaving the door open. He pushed it wider. "Welcome."

The hallway, laid with gleaming wood, went the length of the house. There was a staircase near the front door and large rooms off the hall. It was gorgeous.

"Head on back to the kitchen." Cody indicated down the hall to the back of the house.

As they made their way there Stacey could tell that it was a functional home with little extras for decoration. It screamed that no woman lived there. In the kitchen, she found a large bar and picture windows through which she could see a porch running the length of the house. There was also a great view of the ocean beyond.

"Girls, let's get what we need together before we go out to check the lobster pots. Jean, you get the fire supplies. Lizzy, the pot, napkins, plates and bowls."

Both went into action. Stacey couldn't help but be impressed. Cody was teaching his girls important lessons like teamwork. "What can I do to help?"

"Uh...how about getting the butter and drinks out of the refrigerator and the bread off the counter?" He pointed to the other side of the room.

A few minutes later the girls headed out the back door, down the steps of the porch and along the path to the water. She and Cody followed with their hands full. He had pulled matches out of a high cabinet, put a roll of brown paper under his arm, located a butcher's knife and picked up a bag of tiny potatoes before he was ready to go.

They continued down the path through the rocks to a small sandy beach where a wooden rowboat sat beached and tied to a pole.

"You run a smooth operation, in and out of the OR, Doctor."

He grinned. "It helps to be doing something they want to do. I can't say that it's always that way."

"They're nice girls. You should be proud." She watched Jean and Lizzy place the things they had on a rock.

"I am. It hasn't always been easy for them." There was a sad note in his voice.

"My guess would be not for you either."

He gave her a wry smile and continued ahead of her. He called, "Girls, get your lifejackets on."

Both girls scrambled to the boat.

Cody put his things down beside the others and turned to her, taking what she held. "Thanks for asking me along. I could tell your heart wasn't in the invitation."

"The girls are right, everyone should experience a lobster bake when they have a chance. I'm glad you agreed to come. Really."

He sounded sincere. "I'm looking forward to seeing how this all works."

"Have you ever been out in a rowboat?" he asked.

"Nope."

"Thankfully it's a calm afternoon so we should have a good trip out and back. We aren't going far. You'll need to put on a lifejacket as well."

They walked to the boat. Cody reached inside and pulled out a lifejacket, handing it to her. While she put hers on, he did the same with one of his own and checked the girls. Stacey was glad she'd worn her windbreaker, her old jeans and canvas shoes. Her evening walk had become an unexpected adventure.

Jean and Lizzy scrambled over the side of the boat and took a seat on a bench in the middle.

"Get in," Lizzy called. "Daddy will push us out."

Stacey looked at Cody. "You don't need my help?"

He gave her a pointed look. "Just have a seat."

She did, taking the small one up front, facing the girls and the back of the boat. They were soon sliding into the water. Cody hopped in with the litheness of an athlete at the last second, keeping his feet dry. He took the bench seat in the back of the boat and picked up the oars. Moving into a rhythmic pull, with determination, he had them out in the water in no time. With skill he turned them around so that he was facing out to the horizon.

Since Stacey faced him she couldn't stop herself from appreciating the flexing of his body as he heaved the water forward. The tendons in his neck rose, making him look more masculine. This type of exercise must have something to do with creating his firm chest. She was staring, but she couldn't help herself.

"We're going out there to where those red and green floats are. Our pots are tied to them. Those are our colors so the lobster fishermen know not to pick them up."

Stacey pulled her attention away from Cody long enough to crane her neck around to see the bobbing buoys behind her, which were large enough to see clearly.

"Hey, you okay?"

She met Cody's gaze, hoping her expression revealed nothing.

"You're not scared, are you?" He was watching her closely. "You do know how to swim?"

Stacey swallowed. "Uh...no. I mean yes. I'm just enjoying the scenery."

His eyes widened slightly, holding a questioning gleam before his lips curved at a rakish angle. "Really?"

Realizing what she'd said, heat as hot as a summer day shot up her neck. Had he thought she'd meant something else by the way she'd been looking at him? Maybe she should jump overboard! She stared at Maple Island behind him instead of his impressive chest. "Yes, really."

Cody's soft chuckle carried over the sound of the water lapping against the boat.

Soon he pulled alongside the first float and Jean grabbed it. Cody quickly brought the oars into the boat and took it from her. Hauling the rope attached to the buoy hand over hand, he brought the pot to the surface.

Stacey held her breath in anticipation. The girls' eyes were glued to the water.

"I bet we've got a big one." Lizzy's voice was filled with excitement.

"It's a little early in the season so I hope we have at least one." Cody continued to work.

"We'll get one, Daddy. You know where to put the pots."

Stacey watched him, grinning. It was nice to hear a child have that much confidence in her parent. Stacey hadn't felt the same about hers. If her father had been around, would she have adored him? She'd never know. "Why, Dr. Brennan, you're a lobsterman as well as a surgeon. Who would have thought?"

He gave her a quick acknowledging look before his attention returned to the job at hand.

The girls were inching toward the side of the boat the pot was on.

"Girls, stay put. We don't want to turn Stacey over. Better yet, move to the other side while I'm getting this up."

"Where do you want me?" Stacey asked.

"You just stay put. If you see the boat dipping too far to one side, then adjust a little."

Stacey had next to zilch experience with boats but she could do that.

Cody continued to lift the square metal cage until it sat on the rim of the boat, with water sloshing through the holes until it was completely out of the water. Cody's thighs were wet now, defining the strength of them.

"Daddy, we got one. We've got one," Lizzy squealed, half-standing.

The greenish-brown crustacean remained secure in the middle of the pot.

Stacey reached over and placed a hand on Lizzy's shoulder, easing her to the bench.

"Well, it looks like at least one of us is going to eat tonight." Cody's broad smile beamed at them each in turn. He placed the pot in the bottom of the boat, sat and picked up the oars once more. The girls' attention remained on the lobster as Cody rowed to the next buoy. Minutes later he came alongside it.

"I'll get it." Stacey reached over the side. Grabbing the buoy then the rope, she hung on as the boat continued to move forward. When the slack was gone it jerked her forward and onto the bottom of the boat, but she continued to clutch the rope.

"You all right?" Cody's concern was clear in both his voice and face. He started over the girls' bench toward her.

"I'm fine. Give me a second and I'll have this trap... uh...pot out of the water." She righted herself by sliding into a sitting position. Tugging, she felt the pot lift off the sea bottom. Slowly she drew the rope up. Her shoulders burned.

When she started to stand Cody called, "Don't! You might go over. You're doing great. Just keep at it. It should almost be up."

Seconds later the top of the pot surfaced.

Jean leaned over the side. "You have two. Two!" Her smile went from ear to ear.

"Our best catch ever." Cody sounded as excited as his daughter as he sat as far to one side as he could as a counterbalance to the extra weight. Stacey grabbed the pot.

"Let me see." Lizzy moved to Stacey's side of the boat.

"Hold on a minute. Let's let Stacey get it into the boat. Give her some room."

Stacey pulled it up and over the side until it sat on one end in the bottom of the boat. The process wasn't nearly as effortless as Cody had made it look. She had gotten wetter than him. Yet she smiled triumphantly. "I'm going to get to eat tonight after all."

"That you are." His smile was the one that she liked so much.

"We all are." Jean moved the pot around, laying it down as she gave the lobsters a closer look.

"You're right." Cody picked up the oars again and started pulling them toward the shore.

The return was much faster with the help of the current.

When they reached the sand, Stacey jumped out with

the rope in hand having given up on trying to keep her shoes or clothes dry. She hurried to the pole to secure the boat. Cody hopped over the side, pulling the boat up on the shore. He then lifted Lizzy out. Jean handed him one lobster pot then the other before he assisted her.

"We need to get the fire going, girls." Cody tied off the pots so that the lobsters remained in the water. "Go out and scrounge up some driftwood. Think small pieces first."

Jean and Lizzy scampered away in opposite directions.

Stacey watched them with a smile. "What can I do?"

"All we're going to need is a good fire. Have you ever built one?"

She threw her shoulders back and let him see her indignation. "I'll have you know I'm a professional at that. When you live part of your life in different spots all over the world you learn some survival skills."

"Well, all right, Ms. Professional Fire Builder, let's see what you've got."

Getting down on her hands and knees, Stacey scooped out a hole in the sand. With that done, she pulled some paper off the roll Cody had brought down. By that time both the girls had returned with kindling-size driftwood. "Now run and get some larger pieces and we'll soon have this fire blazing."

Jean and Lizzy took off.

"Hey," she said over her shoulder to Cody, "do you have those matches?"

He sat the large boiler he'd filled with water down next to the fire pit and dug into his vest pocket, bringing out a small box of matches. Her hand brushed his as she took them. Awareness shot through her. Her hands shook as she tried to strike one.

"If we're going to have cooked lobster then we're going to need a fire, Ms. Professional Fire Starter. Do you need my help?"

Stacey took a stabilizing breath. She could do this. Leaning close to the paper, she struck another match and the paper and kindling caught fire. "I've got this."

Cody grinned. "I see that."

The girls returned with their arms full and dropped the wood on the ground. Stacey added pieces and they soon had a roaring fire. Standing, she stretched the kinks out of her muscles. She glanced at Cody. Their gazes met for a moment.

Jean called, "Daddy, put the pot on."

He hesitated a moment before turning away to pick up the boiler and carefully place it over the fire. "It'll take a few minutes to boil."

"What do we do now?" Stacey was enjoying this adventure more than she had anticipated.

"We need to set the table." Cody picked up the roll of paper and opened it across the ground.

"We're going to eat on that?" Stacey looked at his arrangement in amazement.

"Yep. Jean, you want to help me with the lobster?" He handed Stacey a small metal bowl and the stick of butter on his way to the boat. "Will you put the bowl near the fire so it'll melt?"

Stacey did as he asked, aware of Lizzy watching.

Soon Cody and Jean returned with a lobster pot carried between them. "We'll get this one in then go get the other two." Pulling heavy gloves on, Cody removed the lobster.

"Watch the pinchers, Daddy. You know what happened last time." Jean moved to stand beside him as if she planned to protect him.

"What happened?" Stacey really wanted to know. To be included in the shared story within this close-knit family. She had so few stories of her own with her family. What family? She only had her mother. They had never really been a family like Cody and his girls were. She always missed that.

"Daddy forgot his gloves and tried to get the lobster out without them. It pinched the end of his finger and he danced around."

Both girls giggled while Stacey laughed.

"It hurt." Cody sounded pitiful, but he smiled.

"It was so funny." For once Jean appeared happy and her age instead of older than her years.

"You can see I didn't forget them this time. I left them in the boat, so I'd have them close."

Stacey grinned. "I can see it now in the papers: *'Eminent surgeon loses finger to lobster.'*"

"Funny, very funny. If you're not careful, you might not get to eat."

Right now, Cody was nothing like the uptight, humorless and far too serious doctor she'd first met. She liked this guy. Really liked him.

Lizzie came to sit beside Stacey, crossing her legs. When Cody held the lobster over the boiling pot, Lizzy clutched Stacey's arm. "Oh, this is the part I don't like."

"Why not?" Stacey searched Lizzy's stricken face.

"Because the lobster cries." She put her hands over her ears.

Cody lowered the lobster into the pot. Soon a small keening filled the air.

Stacey wrinkled up her nose and twisted her mouth. "That is bad." She covered her ears.

"Well, well, well, such a tender heart." Cody had leaned close so that she had no trouble hearing him. "You don't flinch at the sight of blood but you're sympathetic to a lobster." His low chuckle rolled through her, leaving behind a lovely warmth.

They all watched the pot for a few minutes then Cody pronounced, "It's time for this one to come out."

"How do you know?" Stacey asked.

"When it turns red." Jean's tone implied that anyone should know that.

Cody picked up tongs, reached into the pot and pulled out the lobster. Giving it a gentle shake, he placed it on the paper. "Don't touch. It'll still be too hot." He opened the bag of tiny potatoes and dumped them in the pot. "Jean, let's go get the other two."

His daughter didn't hesitate, slipping her hand into her father's larger one. It was a sweet picture, one that Stacey had never experienced with her own father. Shaking off the morose thought, she watched them return with the second pot. Was Jean afraid she might lose her father like she had her mother? What was the real story about Cody's wife?

They returned and set the trap down. She and Lizzy considered the lobsters. One of them was missing a claw.

"What happened?" Stacey asked no one in particular.

"They get in fights when sharing space." Cody picked up the lobster. "This one lost." He unceremoniously dropped that one and then the other into the water.

Once again Lizzie covered her ears, and Stacey joined her. Cody was wearing one of those spectacular smiles she rarely had a glimpse of. The one that made her stomach flutter. When the lobsters were done he lifted them out. He then dumped the water, saving the potatoes. Those he poured out onto the paper. "Stacey, would you please get the butter?"

She did and placed it on the paper as well. He sat on the ground and the girls joined him around the paper "table." Stacey took her spot. Cody reached for the cans of drink and handed one to each of them. Next, he picked up one of the lobsters, removed its head then, using the knife, sliced it down the middle of the back. Pulling the meat from the tail, he halved it and gave a piece to Jean and the other to Lizzy.

He picked up another and waggled it at her. "Do you want to do the honors or shall I?"

"Let me have a try." Stacey reached for the lobster.

"Figures. Is there anything you won't try?"

Stacey looked directly at him. "I try to stay open to new things."

He raised a brow, his gaze not leaving hers as he handed her the lobster.

She clenched her jaw as she twisted the head off, following his example. Handing the body to Cody, she waited while he sliced it open and returned it.

"Here, dip it in the butter." Jean pushed the bowl toward her.

Stacey did as Jean suggested then put the white meat into her month. "Mmm…" A rivulet of butter ran down her chin. "Wipe." She waved a hand in a *give me, give me* motion.

"Be still and I'll get it." Using a napkin, Cody caught the stream before it dripped onto her jacket.

Her gaze jumped to his. Her breaths came in jerks as if she had been running. Among all the men in the world, why did this one affect her so? Why did she let him? It had to stop. "May I have my own napkin?"

Cody pulled back as if rejected. Dismay filled her. She hadn't meant to sound so harsh. But they were becoming too easy with each other. She was being sucked into his world. Even worse, she liked it. But she didn't belong here. Had no experience with a real family.

Reaching beside him, he snagged a napkin and thrust it in her direction.

"Thanks."

"Daddy, my hair is getting in the way." With a messy hand Lizzy pushed the mass of hair that had slipped from the band.

"Scoot around this way and I'll fix it for you," Stacey offered.

"I'll get it." Cody moved to stand.

"Stacey can do it." Lizzy turned her back to Stacey. Cleaning her hands with her napkin, she brought the girl's hair under control.

Lizzy twisted around and studied her with unnerving intensity. "You'd be a good mommy."

"We already have a mommy," Jean announced in a flat tone.

The painful silence was broken when Cody said, "Girls, you need to eat. It's getting dark."

The rest of the meal revolved around finishing it. Done, they all pitched in to clean up.

Amazed, Stacey watched Cody roll what was left of the meal and any garbage in the paper and throw it on the fire. The rest of the stuff he dropped into the pot, including the empty drink cans. "Best clean-up job I've ever seen."

Looking pleased with her praise, he confessed, "I'll

admit this is the easiest meal I cook. Jean, Lizzy, grab an armload and head for the house."

The girls did as he requested and were soon on their way up the path.

Stacey picked up the pot. "You're making great memories for them." What had made her say or think something like that? She knew nothing about making family memories, especially good ones. There were only a few in her childhood that would even measure up to the worth-remembering mark. Still, it was nice to know that even though the girls didn't have their mother, they could still have a happy life. Cody was doing all he could to make that happen.

"I hope so." He kicked sand over the fire, putting it out and filling the hole.

They walked in the direction of the house. "I know this is none of my business…" Stacey glanced over her shoulder to judge his reaction to her next words "…but I can't help wondering what happened with their mother."

Cody wasn't surprised Stacey had asked about Rachael. If he had learned anything in the last week it was that Stacey was forthright. She wouldn't go behind his back and ask others about his life. When there was something she wanted to know she would go to the source and she didn't beat around the bush.

That didn't mean he wanted to talk about Rachael. The subject still left him feeling sick and unsure. Guilt nagged at him when he thought of her. Still, there was something about Stacey that made him want to confide in her. Wanted her to understand him. Why he was the way he was.

"My ex-wife and I were college sweethearts. We had

planned the perfect life together. She'd take care of the home and children and I would be a great surgeon. Give my children what I'd had as a child. A secure home with two parents who loved them. During our senior year she was in a horrible car crash that damaged her ankle and foot. After the initial surgery she went through physical therapy but was still in a lot of pain. There were more surgeries but she finally began to recover. At the end of my med-school years, she walked down the aisle on our wedding day without a limp and I believed that our world had righted itself."

He hated to voice this next part out loud. The misery of that time strangled him. "But for a long time she hid a huge secret. She was addicted to painkillers."

Stacey sucked in a breath. She stopped walking and faced him. "She must have hidden it well."

"She was a functional addict. Jean had already come along when I found out. I got Rachael help and I thought things were better. By the time I found out differently, Lizzy was on the way." He hesitated, the memories making him feel momentarily queasy. "During my residency I was working twenty-four and sometimes forty-eight hours straight. I couldn't keep an eye on her all the time. Mother helped out but it was still hard. What really brought things to a head was when I found a prescription pad missing. Rachael denied she took it but I know she did."

"Oh, Cody, what a nightmare."

He nodded his gratitude skyward, only to focus on Stacey's compassionate face. "Yeah, and I had this perfect life all planned out. Nothing about that time was perfect. My career was on the line. My marriage was dying a painful death and my girls needed at least one good parent. Rachael was crying out for help I couldn't give her."

"What about rehab?"

"Oh, she would break her heart, swearing she would stop, then go to rehab but check herself out early. That happened more than once. It took me over a year of documentation and being overseen by strangers to get full custody of the girls. A few months after that happened, Alex and I met and shared our woes. You know the rest of that story."

Stacey put a hand on his forearm. Thankfully there was no pity in her words when she said, "I'm sorry. I had no idea. I shouldn't have pried."

For some reason it had felt good to tell her. Outside his parents and Alex he'd never discussed what he'd been through. Maybe it was knowing Stacey would only be around for a short period of time that had made the difference. She was here, he had spilled his ugly secret and she would carry it off with her to Ethiopia in a few weeks. Whatever the reason, it felt good to give voice to it. His shoulders felt lighter than they had been in years. He could take a breath.

"Do the girls ever see their mom?"

Cody moved toward the house again. "No. She's in California somewhere. Not even her parents are sure where she is."

"Oh." Stacey slowly followed.

"You can tell Jean has some memory of her. Lizzy doesn't. After I got custody we moved here for a new start. Jean is working through her issues with a help of a therapist. Soon she'll be old enough to fully understand about her mother."

"I'm sure you'll do the right thing when the time comes."

"Don't give me credit where it isn't due. I failed my wife and my girls for a time."

"But you're making it up to them." She continued up the path and climbed the porch steps before she looked back at him. "You're an okay guy, Dr. Brennan."

Cody joined her.

She patted his shoulder. "You're a good dad. You do what you can to give them a nice safe life. They're happy, sweet girls."

"I appreciate you saying that, but it doesn't make the ugliness they started out with go away."

"No, but you're slowly replacing those ugly memories with good ones. Not all children are given a second chance like yours have had." She headed into the house before he had a chance to ask about that wistful note in her voice.

The girls were waiting for them in the kitchen. "It's time for a bath and bed," Cody told them.

Not surprisingly, Lizzy whined, "Do we have to? I wanted Stacey to stay and play a game."

Stacey shook her head. "I can't tonight. I need to be going home. Bye, Jean."

"Bye." There was no warmth in Jean's response.

It didn't matter. She wouldn't be around long enough that Jean should care. But would she treat every woman Cody brought around the same way? Would Jean always yearn for something she didn't have, like *she* had?

"Now head on up," he ordered. "I'll be along to check on you in a few minutes."

"That's my cue to find the door." Stacey put the pot in the sink then walked down the hall to the front of the house. Cody followed her. At the door, she turned to him. "Thanks for the lobster experience. It was fun. I'll have a nice memory too."

"You're welcome. I'm glad you joined us." He meant that. Without thinking, his hands went to rest lightly on her waist. It felt really good to touch her. Their gazes locked.

She inhaled sharply and went stock still.

Did it really surprise her that he would want to kiss her? Was she honestly unaware of how appealing she was? "I know this is a bad idea on so many levels," he murmured, his head moving closer. "You are a colleague. I promised myself I wouldn't bring anyone into my girls' lives who wasn't staying for the long haul. Yet along came you."

His lips met hers. So delicious. Tender, yielding. Perfect. He wanted more.

Stacey pushed him away. "Don't," she commanded. "We can't do this." She opened the door and hurried out.

He watched her blend into the evening shadows. Their kiss had been too short, only leaving him longing for more. A feeling, heavy like a cold wet blanket, hung over him. He wanted Stacey but he'd learned the hard way that there were other considerations in his life that frequently overrode his own wishes.

CHAPTER FOUR

ON WEDNESDAY MORNING, Stacey took a deep breath and knocked on Cody's office door. It was time for rounds. She hadn't seen him for the last two days. He'd been in Boston both mornings, doing small repair surgeries on the senator's son. He'd said she wasn't needed there, but he wanted her to see the patients at the clinic for him.

After her rejection of his parting kiss, she wasn't sure what her reception would be. She shouldn't have gone with him to the beach. Shouldn't have put either one of them in that position. More than once she'd tried to say no but had given in anyway. Now things would be strained between them. She didn't need that, even if she was only around for two and a half more weeks.

The time she had spent with Cody and the girls had been the best she'd experienced in a long time. For just a little while she'd been a part of a family. And she'd liked it too well. It wasn't a good idea for her or for Cody and his girls to get too involved with each other. Still, she couldn't help herself. Growing up in a family had been all she'd wanted, to really belong somewhere.

Trepidation filled her. Would Cody want to talk about their kiss? She was likely making too big a deal out of it. After all his lips had barely touched hers. So why couldn't she get it out of her mind? She briefly brushed her bottom lip with a finger. She remembered every second of his touch, the press of his firm mouth against hers. It probably hadn't been as memorable for Cody. In spite of herself, she wanted a chance at trying it again. She'd bet he could really curl her toes if she gave him half a chance. But she wouldn't let that happen. Couldn't.

At the sound of his "Come in," she stuck her head around the door. Cody sat behind a large oak desk that looked as if it was an antique.

"I'm ready to do rounds when you are." She couldn't step any further into his space for fear her resolve would slip.

He glanced up. "Okay. Give me another sec here." Cody looked down again. "Come in and sit down. We need to talk anyway."

Great. That wasn't what she wanted to do. But she had no choice. How foolish would she look if she refused to talk to the man she worked for? She was trying to forget their kiss and them hashing it out wasn't going to help that happen.

She took one of the two overstuffed chairs in front of his desk. It should be against the law for a man to look so attractive when doing nothing more than sitting at his desk. Heaven help her, she was losing her mind.

Cody clicked a key then looked at her. "I just wanted to let you know what's going to happen."

Her heart pounded. *Happen?* Between them?

"The senator's son is going to be moved out here the day after tomorrow."

Relief, quickly followed by disappointment, washed over her. She needed to focus. If she'd worried Cody might have felt something after their kiss she had just been assured he hadn't. "Um, okay. I'll see that the paper-work is in order."

"Good. See it gets to Harborside Hospital. The boy will be doing physical therapy here and will need a cou-ple more small surgeries when he has healed enough. I'll also need you to run point with his parents as well as any reporters they require you to respond to."

"Shouldn't you be the one to speak to the reporters?" She didn't do well with being in front of people. The thought of talking on TV struck her heart with terror.

Apparently that was evident on her face because Cody asked, "You don't like that idea?"

"Not at all."

"Why not?"

"I don't do public speaking." She wrung her hands in her lap.

Cody crossed his arms, leaned them on his desk and watched her with those amazing all-seeing chocolate eyes.

Stacey squirmed.

He said with slow emphasis, "You mean there's some-thing in this world that you're afraid of? Who would have thought?"

Was he making fun of her? She sat straighter. Grip-ping the arms of the chair, she said, "I'll have you know I'm afraid of a number of things." *Like you not kissing me again.*

"I haven't seen it. If you're uncomfortable with any-thing to do with the reporters just let me know. As a general rule security will handle almost anything. The reporters know we put a high priority on protecting our patients' privacy. For the most part they leave us alone."

Cody sat back. "That being said, if the senator's son's

history is any indication, I don't anticipate him being one of our easiest patients. So don't say I didn't give you fair warning."

"I can handle him."

"There's that confidence I was looking for." He grinned. "If there's anything you question or are not one hundred percent sure about, you can certainly run it past me first. I'll be putting him in a semi-private room instead of a private one. His parents probably won't like the idea, but he'll be busy feeling sorry for himself and I want him to work at getting better while he is here. If for no other reason than he wants to get away from his roommate. No lying around in his bed all day."

Stacey was impressed. Cody wasn't only thinking about his patient's physical well-being but his mental health as well. "I'll see that he gets a particularly irritating roommate."

Cody smiled. "Good thinking." He pushed back from the desk. "Let's get the rounds done. It's dance night for the girls."

"Don't sound so excited." She stood and headed toward the door.

He joined her. "I have to admit it's the hardest night of the week. You really saved me last week. If you hadn't shared your booth with us at the bistro, I would've been there waiting for ages with two whiny girls on a school night. Not my idea of fun. I owe you."

They walked up the hall toward the patients' rooms.

"I had payback with that lobster dinner you gave me on Sunday." She pushed her hair out of the way to see him better. "You want me to go to the bistro again and save you a table tonight?" She was kidding but what if he took her seriously? Her goal was to put space between them, not see him more often.

He stopped at the room door of Alonso, the tennis star whose knee he had repaired the week before. "I don't think that'll be necessary."

She was glad to hear it.

Knocking, he then pushed the door open to see the room empty of tennis stars. He looked back at her. "Where is he?"

"This time of the day I bet he's in the community room. He likes to listen to Salty tell the twins stories."

They moved on up the hall.

"So, you have met Connor and Peyton Walsh?"

"Yeah, they're hard to miss. Cute kids. Really nice parents."

"It has been tough on them with their children both being hurt. But the twins are recovering well and should be going home soon. They've kind of become the clinic mascots."

"Well, it's testament to you and Alex that you guys decided early on that you'd save some beds for those who couldn't afford the clinic and take care of the locals. You two are good guys."

"Hey, don't be putting me on a pedestal because I can guarantee I'll fall."

Did he really think that little of himself? From what she'd seen, he was almost perfect. Almost too good to be true. "I'm sure it wouldn't be far if you did."

Cody glanced at her in a doubtful manner. "Thanks."

She shouldn't have said that. Her mouth was always getting her into trouble. Even their conversations should remain impersonal.

As if he didn't like the direction of their exchange either, he said, "Alonso decided that he would recover faster here at the clinic. That way he would be able to stay out of the media spotlight for a while longer. It's also easier to do the rehab without coming over daily on the ferry."

She whispered, "I've heard that more than one famous person has hidden out here. Want to share who?"

"Nope, and we like to refer to it as recovering." He mimicked her low tone.

The sound made her shiver inside. What would it be like to have him whisper to her like that as they made love? No, that was no place for her mind to go. She swallowed. "Aw, got it."

He stopped and looked at her before he said, "I thought Alonso might be the person to put the senator's son in with but I've thought better of it."

Stacey gave him a wry smile. "I'm thinking Salty might be the best choice."

Cody nodded. "I think you might be right. He will certainly be able to hold his own with the unhappy teen. And since Salty's here for only a few more days of observation and IV antibiotics, neither one of them will have time to kill the other off. Philomena will be here to referee. She isn't going to let anything happen to Salty."

"It's sweet."

"Salty isn't sweet."

"No, but the fact that Mrs. Kerridge-Bates and Salty can find love after all these years is. Especially since they're so different."

Cody gave her a narrowed-eye look. "I wouldn't have ever taken you for a romantic."

Was she? She didn't believe in happily ever after for herself, but she did like to see others achieve it. She shrugged. "We all have our off days."

They visited two more patients before going to the community room in search of Alonso. He was there. Salty was surrounded by him, the twins and a few other patients.

"Hey, there, Connor and Peyton. You two look like you are doing well." Cody greeted them.

"Hi, Dr. Brennan."

"So, what's this group up to today?" Cody looked from Salty to Alonso and then to the twins.

"We've just been listening to stories." The twins looked at Salty with nothing short of hero-worship.

"Your mom and daddy coming in this evening?" Cody asked.

"Mom is. Dad has to work again." Peyton fiddled with a string on her shirt.

Stacey couldn't help but feel sorry for the twins. They had been at the clinic for too long.

"How're you feeling, Salty?" Cody asked.

"He'd feel much better if he'd stop holding court and rest more," a gruff but caring female voice said behind them.

They all looked toward Philomena, who was shuffling in using a walker.

"Philly thinks she should run my life," Salty grumbled. "Where I'd really like to be is off on my boat."

"Not until you're completely well this time." Philly sat in a chair beside him. "I'm too old to worry all the time."

Stacey didn't miss him touching her hand for a second. They cared about each other more than they let on. What would it be like to have that type of connection with someone? She glanced at Cody. A girl could dream.

"Sorry to interrupt but, Alonso, can I have a look at your incision sites?" Cody asked.

The young man turned in his chair and pulled up his knit pants above his knee.

"They look good," Cody confirmed. "How's the physical therapy going?"

"Well, I think I'll be better than ever on the court." Alonso sounded pleased with his progress. "Thanks, Doc. I wouldn't be this far along without you."

Cody lowered his head in a humble gesture. "You've done most of the work."

How like Cody. It was nice to work in a place with quality care and excellent doctors who weren't full of self-importance. Stacey glanced at him again. Also, with devoted doctors. If she wasn't careful she'd move from admiration straight into the hero-worship he had already warned her about.

A few minutes later she and Cody left the community room. He headed down the hall in the opposite direction from the one she took. "Stacey."

She stopped and turned. Had he forgotten to tell her something? "Yes?"

He stepped closer. "I…uh…wanted to apologize about the other night. I stepped over the line. It won't happen again."

Here it was. What she'd been dreading but had thought by now wouldn't come up. "It's okay." She lowered her voice. "It's nothing against you. I just don't think it's a good idea for us to get involved."

"I agree."

He did? Her chest ached with regret. She shouldn't feel that way. Didn't she want him to agree? Protecting her heart was the priority. She was a short-term girl and he was a forever man. They would never work as a couple.

Neither of them spoke as a nurse passed by.

"Then I guess there's nothing more to say." Stacey forced a smile to her lips.

He watched her for a moment before he said, "I have to get the girls."

Cody had mulled the problem over for a couple of days now, trying to figure out what to do. He was attracted to his nurse. So much so that Stacey consumed almost all of his thoughts. Maybe it was because he couldn't have her. Or it could just be because he'd been without a woman so long that anyone who showed him any attention appealed. Whatever it was, it had to stop. Seeing her every day didn't help. He'd taken to counting the hours until Stacey left the island. At least then he would have some peace of sorts.

She wasn't a woman he needed to bring any further into his life. She already fit too well. His girls liked her too much. Like sunshine after the dark, Stacey added light to his world. She had been open and giving with his girls and they didn't need to grow attached to someone who would be leaving them soon. Still, the need to get to know her, have her, gnawed at him. He just had to live through it for a couple of more weeks and then the problem would be solved for him.

He'd just finished surgery and spoken to the family when she came up beside him. Without speaking, they walked to his office to finish some paperwork she needed to discharge a patient. Once again, he would be alone with her.

She'd remained all business since his apology, which both helped and maddened him. He couldn't think straight when she was around, especially when she came close enough that he caught her scent.

She gave him a curious look. "Hey, what's bothering you?"

Cody glanced at her. Did she really know him well enough to recognize when something was disturbing him? Was he that transparent or had she been watching him closely enough to learn his moods? He wasn't sure he liked either idea. Should he tell her? He sighed. No, that wasn't going to happen. He'd find something else to say.

"It's not that big a deal."

"It must be something because you've been… I don't know…preoccupied the last two days."

He huffed, giving her the only excuse he could come up with. "The girls need costumes for Founder's Day. And the worst part is they need to be home-made. They have a dress rehearsal on Wednesday." It might sound stupid but it was a very real problem he'd been struggling with whenever he could get his mind off her. Even better, he didn't have to admit the real reason he was acting out of the norm—his battle to not kiss her whenever they were alone, which was far too often for his peace of mind.

"And this is a problem why?"

His arms went wide with his palms up. "Because I have nothing. Nothing. No ideas. No capability or even the desire to do it."

She actually laughed at him. Doubled over with it. Between gasping breaths, she said, "The super-dad is undone by costumes."

"It's not funny." He stalked into his office. At least being mildly irritated with her made him stop thinking about grabbing her and kissing her for all of a minute.

"No, it's not. I'm sorry I'm making fun of you. Would you like me to help?"

Stacey had actually offered that after their "discussion." She had made it clear they shouldn't get mixed up in each other's personal lives. Had she changed her mind? Whether she had or hadn't wasn't important. He could use her help. Should he accept her offer? She had said she liked to dress up. Surely she had some skills in that area. The girls had to have outfits.

The only women he knew who might help were already busy. Maggie had her hands full with Jake. Fleur was running the show so she didn't have time to take care of his girls. He probably could ask Brigid Brady from the bistro, but she'd expect more from him than he was interested in giving. Stacey was offering, and he was definitely interested in what she might expect of him in return.

He hesitated a moment longer but couldn't think of another choice he had. "Would you, please? Getting costumes together is not in my wheelhouse. Even buying them in a store gives me the hives but the idea of coming up with them on my own makes me want to pull my hair out." He sounded pathetic even to his own ears.

Stacey continued to grin. "Little dramatic, aren't you? You've convinced me, if not for you, then for the girls. What are they supposed to wear?"

"They need to dress like children of the historical period. You know, dresses or just something that's easy but along that line. Remember me, that 'no ideas' guy?"

She chuckled. He didn't appreciate being laughed at, but he did enjoy the sound of her laughter. When it subsided she nodded. "Okay. When's a good time for me to see the girls?"

"I don't expect you to do it by yourself. I can help." He winced. "With some guidance." He pushed the door to his office open. "I hate to take up your time off but

being Saturday tomorrow, the girls are also free—afternoon would be the best."

"I'll be at your house at three. Does that work for
you all?"

"It does. I'll try to have what the girls already own out
for you to look at. Give you somewhere to start."

With great relief on two levels, Cody watched her
leave his office a few minutes later. One, that someone
else would be organizing costumes for his girls and, two,
that Stacey was no longer standing so intimately close to
him. He fisted his hands. Her scent still hung in the air.

Stacey arrived at Cody's house the next day right on
three. She was sure she was making a mistake by becoming further involved in Cody's life. For a moment
there yesterday she'd feared he would swoop her up into
his arms when she'd offered to help him.

She knocked on the front door. Seconds later there
was the sound of feet running before the door opened
and Lizzy stood there with a grin. Behind her was Cody.
He wore a pullover sweater with a T-shirt beneath, jeans
and socks. An unsure smile covered his lips.

She shivered. Was she missing something?

Lizzy pulled on her hand. "Come on. We have to go
upstairs."

Stacey looked up to see Jean standing on the stairs.
"Hi."

Jean quietly said, "Hi."

"Lizzy, let's give Stacey a chance to come in." Cody
brushed Stacey's back with his arm as he reached to close
the door. She had no doubt it was unintentional but that
didn't stop her body from reacting. She'd made a huge
mistake by coming here. Why had she opened her big

mouth and suggested she help them? Because Cody had looked so pitiful and she'd been unable to stop herself from volunteering her talents. Or resist the opportunity to be a part of his family just once more before she left them behind forever. It was nice to feel needed, valued.

"How're you?" he asked, as if he really wanted to know.

"I'm good." She looked at Jean again who had come further down the stairs. "I'm ready to get started on costumes. How about you, girls?"

"Better you than me," Cody muttered.

Stacey smiled. "I figured you'd think that."

"The girls have already gone through some of their clothes and put out things that you might be able to use. I apologize for the state of their rooms."

Stacey started toward the stairs. "No problem. We'll see what they have."

"Let's go." Lizzy pulled on her hand. "This way."

Jean climbed the stairs and she and Lizzy followed. Stacey looked back at Cody, who followed them up. His brows were in a V of concern at the bridge of his nose. She grinned. "Don't worry. I've got this."

He gave her a quizzical look. "You sure?"

"Positive."

On the landing at the top of the stairs, Stacey stopped. "How about we start with you, Jean?"

She stood inside a doorway. "Okay."

Stacey followed her into the room. It was decorated a bright yellow. "Wow, what a pretty room."

Cody moved to sit in a chair in the corner, out of the way.

Jean gave her a slight smile and looked at Cody. "Daddy let me pick the color."

Stacey wasn't surprised. Cody loved his girls and wanted to make them happy. "Let's see what you've got here. I found a picture of what you need to look like on the internet. Do you girls have any boots? Maybe rubber ones? You know, the kind you wear in the snow?"

"They do," Cody said.

Jean ran to the closet and returned with black boots. "Perfect."

"I have some too," Lizzy confirmed.

"Great." Stacey ruffled her hair. "Then you can wear yours as well. Now for dresses. Let's see what we have here." Stacey looked through the clothes that were all topsy-turvy on the bed then turned to the closet. There she found a dress with long sleeves and would hang below Jean's knees. Stacey held it up. "I think this might do. Jean, would you put it on with your boots?"

The entire time she was working with the clothes she felt Cody watching her. She glanced up to confirm it. His dark look didn't waver. "Jean, have your dad help you." Maybe with Cody having something to do he wouldn't have time to make her feel self-conscious.

"While you do that, Lizzy and I are going to see if we can find something for her. Lizzy, how about showing me to your room?"

The child skipped out of the room and down the hall. Stacey couldn't help but like the girls. They'd had a hard start in life but were pleasant children. Jean still hadn't warmed up to her but that didn't matter. It was even better that way. If she did, it would just make it that much harder for both of them when Stacey had to leave.

The girls' bedrooms were side by side and they shared a bathroom. Lizzy's room was blue and done in what

Stacey guessed was a theme from her favorite cartoon show. Clothes were spread everywhere in there as well.

On the floor Stacey found a dress similar to Jean's and held it up. "This should do. Lizzy, will you put this on? And your boots."

She was in the process of removing her shirt when Stacey turned around. Jean had entered the room. "Why, Jean, you look great. All we have to do now is find you an apron, collar and head covering." Lizzy was having trouble pulling her dress over her head and Stacey stepped over to help. "Now, what can we use for collars? Do you girls have any white scarves?"

"I might have a couple," Cody said from the doorway.

Lizzy gave her a perplexed look "Scarf?"

"You know, Lizzy. The kind Daddy wears when he's going to an important meeting when it snows."

"I know where those are." Lizzy shot out of the room, her boots slapping against the wood floor.

"Wait, Lizzy, I'll get them," Cody called.

Jean shot by her, going after Lizzy and Cody.

Stacey followed more slowly. She stopped in the doorway of a spacious bedroom overlooking the back of the house. A wide bed faced a picture window framing a beautiful view of the ocean. There was a sitting area that included a TV and desk. On another wall was a chest of drawers.

Cody was looking through the top drawer of the chest. He pulled out a scarf with an air of triumph. He looked at her. "Will this do?"

"I believe so."

Jean joined Lizzy beside Cody. "Is there one for me?" She considered her father expectantly.

Cody pulled out another one. "Back up, girls, and let Stacey do her thing. She's the one with the plan."

All three of them turned to her with *now what?* expressions on their faces.

"They go around your neck. The ends can be tucked inside your dresses." She hadn't moved from the doorway.

"You *can* come in." Cody's voice held a hint of humor.

Still Stacey hesitated. If she did, she was entering his personal space, the forbidden land. Even with the girls there it filled her with naughty anticipation. As if she were entering a place of excitement and danger. She refused to let him see that. "I know." Taking a deep breath, she walked toward them. As innocent as the reason was, she was still in Cody's bedroom. She looked around. It would be the one and only time.

Cody's gaze remained on hers as she came toward him. What was he thinking? Anything near her own thoughts? No, she'd made it clear the other night and again in the hallway of the clinic that she wouldn't allow anything to happen between them. But had she really meant it? Had he accepted it?

Jean handed her a scarf. "Do mine first."

Stacey blinked, her focus shifting to the eight-year-old. That was good. She had to quit thinking about Cody. Taking the scarf, she wrapped it around Jean's neck, tucked the ends into her dress then fluffed it out around her neck. Standing back, she looked at her handiwork. "You're starting to look like a real Pilgrim girl."

"My turn," Lizzy cried.

Stacey did the same with her scarf. Done, she said, "Now we need to find you each an apron." She turned to Cody. "Do you have any aprons in the kitchen?"

"Are you kidding?" he croaked. "Never use them."

"Figures." She looked around the room. "What can we use?" She pursed her lips in thought. A slow grin formed on her lips. She snapped her fingers. "Got it." She looked at Cody. "I'm not sure you're going to like this."

He took a step back. "What?"

"I need a couple of your white dress shirts."

"Are you going to cut them up?" He sounded horrified at the idea.

She grinned. "No, but they may take some wear and tear."

His chin drew back and he narrowed his eyes, looking unsure. "Okay, I guess."

The girls whooped and ran for the door. They soon returned, each with a shirt in hand.

Cody's eyes widened and his brows rose.

"There a problem?" Stacey asked, standing beside him.

"Those look like my very best shirts."

She giggled. Cody looked at her. His eyes sparkled and she wasn't certain why but a hot spot formed in her belly in response.

"Here." Lizzy thrust the one she held at Stacey. Jean did the same.

"What're we going to do with them?" Jean asked.

"Come over here and I'll show you." Stacey moved to the bed. Not one of her better ideas but she was left no choice but to follow through. Laying the shirt across the bedspread, she buttoned it up completely. She then flipped it over and smoothed the wrinkles out. What would it be like to do this while Cody was wearing it? She shook that pulse-raising idea out of her head. Folding the collar down, she rolled the shirt tightly past the shoulders.

Cody groaned.

She glanced at him.

"My shirts will never be the same."

Stacey grinned. "You're the one who asked for my help."

He winced. "I did."

"Okay, Jean. Turn around." When she did so, Stacey adjusted the shirt so that the buttons faced inward then tied the sleeves at Jean's back. "Okay, you can turn around." Jean did so, and Stacey said with arms wide in a theatrical pose, "Ta-da."

Jean had a genuine smile on her face.

"Do mine now," Lizzy said.

Stacey started on the other shirt.

Cody watched over her shoulder. "I have to admit this is pretty creative. I'm impressed."

"You doubted me?" She looked at him.

"Not really."

Having male support was a new experience for her. Stacey rather liked Cody's faith in her. She tied Lizzy's "apron" on. "I believe we have two original settlers. Stand over there so your dad and I can see you."

The girls did as they were told with smiles on their faces.

Stacey twirled a finger. "Turn around for us."

The girls did.

"You two look great." Cody nodded, his relief evident. "Thanks, Stacey. I would have never come up with this."

"You're welcome, but we still have something missing." She snapped her fingers. "I meant to bring my old hat. I can go get it."

"I'm afraid that will have to wait for now. I have a Founder's Day meeting in a few minutes." He clapped his hands. "Girls, we've already taken too much of Stacey's time. Lucy is expecting you at her sleepover party."

Jean wrinkled her nose. "But we need to finish our costumes first."

Stacey put a hand on her shoulder. "I'll work on your head covering while you're gone and have it ready for you. Now, let's take those outfits off and keep them safe. It sounds like you have a party to go to."

With her help and Cody's, they changed.

"Go put your regular clothes on, girls. We've got to go," Cody encouraged.

Stacey helped Cody lay the clothing neatly on the chair at his desk. He placed the "aprons" just so and the boots beside them with great care. "I don't want anything to happen to these between now and when they need to use them. I hope I can get it all on them correctly."

"I'm sure you can but if you need me to come help, let me know." The offer came out of her mouth as though it had a mind of its own. She had to stop saying things like that. Getting more and more deeply involved in Cody's life wasn't her plan. It wasn't until they were done that she registered she was alone with him in his bedroom.

His voice dropped and he touched her hand briefly, sending a ripple throughout her body. "Thanks for helping me out. For that I'll always be indebted to you."

She stepped out of touching distance. "I'm not helping you to make you feel you owe me anything."

"I know that. You're not that kind of person. Still, I'm grateful." His eyes filled with an emotion she didn't want to put a name to. "Stacey, I—"

"We're ready to go," Lizzy announced from the doorway. Jean stood behind her, watching closely.

Cody retreated, his unfinished statement lingering in the air. Stacey desperately wanted to know what he'd been going to say while at the same time feared it. "Girls, what do we say to Stacey?"

"Thank you," they choroused.

Stacey smiled. "You're very welcome."

"Jean and Lizzy, get your overnight bag and go get in the car. Buckle up." The girls followed his orders. Soon the stomping of their feet filled the air as they went down the stairs.

Cody stopped her from following them with a hand on her arm. "Stacey—"

"You don't have to thank me again. I was glad to do it."

"That wasn't what I was going to say."

She made herself meet his unwavering gaze. "What?"

Cody studied her for a second as if unsure. "You know, you really are special." With that he left her alone in his bedroom.

Heat rushed through her. What would it be like to hear those words from his lips all the time? That wasn't a dream she should be having. Cody's life wasn't the one for her. This was just a temporary interlude.

CHAPTER FIVE

CODY ARRIVED HOME a few hours later to a house that was too quiet. The girls didn't often spend the night away and when they did he was usually gone himself. He'd never thought much about being lonely until now. Lizzy and Jean had been his whole world for years but somehow Stacey had stepped into it and he was starting to ask himself if he needed more in his life.

She brought warmth and laughter to his world. Being around her had him feeling things he'd not felt in a long time. He was excited to wake in the mornings. Not until Stacey had he realized he had been living on autopilot. He would miss her teasing and quick smiles when she left for Ethiopia. That left him feeling oddly dejected.

A knock on the front door brought him out of his musing. He opened it to find Stacey standing there.

"Hey, I hope I'm not interrupting but I finished these and I thought Jean and Lizzy would want them as soon as they got home in the morning." She held up two strips of white.

He gave them a peculiar look, trying to figure out what they were. Had she stopped by to see him knowing the girls wouldn't be there?

"They're bonnets. Don't you remember?" She sounded as if she wanted to shake him to get him to answer.

He was still wrapped up in the surprise and pleasure of seeing her again. "Yeah, but isn't there more to them than that?"

She harrumphed. "Sorry. Not. Pilgrims didn't wear much headgear."

He nodded. "If you say so."

She extended her hand, offering the fabric to him. "Well, I'd better go."

He took them from her, his fingers brushing hers. Awareness rippled through him. The impulse to grab her and pull her into his arms ran through his mind but he didn't want to scare her away. The girls weren't there so he didn't have to worry about them becoming any more attached to Stacey. This was just a chance for some time alone with her when it didn't involve work or his children. As a grown man he could deal with the fallout when she was gone. "I was just going to have a bowl of ice cream. Would you like to join me?"

She gave the question more thought than it required. He began to worry she wouldn't accept. "That sounds good to me. Sure."

"Good. Then why don't you come in." He stood back, giving her space.

Stacey grinned at him. "And I was starting to think you might make me eat it on your front stoop."

"Are you questioning my manners?" He narrowed his eyes at her as he grinned before he closed the door.

"It's not my place to question the doctor," she cooed.

He laughed. "Yeah, right. You do that regularly."

She led the way to the kitchen. "I don't think we re-member things the same way."

"I think my memory is just fine." He'd like to give her something to remember him by. Mercy, he needed to get his mind out of the bedroom and back in the kitchen. He hung the bonnets over a doorknob. Maybe he should stick his head in the freezer instead of taking the ice cream out of it.

Stacey took a seat on one of the bar stools. Cody was aware of her watching him. He was sure she wasn't missing a single move he made. It had been a long time since he'd been this unsettled by a woman. He found it both exciting and disconcerting. "Chocolate or vanilla?"

"Both, please."

"Both it is." He took the cartons out of the freezer then retrieved bowls from a cabinet and spoons from a drawer. "Scoop of each?"

"Two scoops chocolate and one vanilla." He looked at her and her gaze didn't waver.

Cody smiled. He was having fun. "You do like ice cream."

"Yes, I do. You offered just the right dessert."

His gaze caught hers. "I have others as well." She blinked. He let her off the hook and filled a bowl and pushed it over to her. Stacey eyed it. "Don't wait on me to get started."

She didn't hesitate before she filled her spoon. "Mmm… this hits the spot."

Cody watched her. He wished he could be the one who had put that look of pleasure on her face. He shook his head. If he didn't get control of his raging emotions he would jump her right here in the kitchen!

He filled his bowl and put the ice cream away before he joined her on a stool next to hers. They ate without any conversation for a few minutes with nothing but the sound of spoons against the bowls. It was a comfortable silence, the kind he'd not shared with another adult in a long time.

"You know, my mother and I always ate ice cream after one of her husbands left," Stacey said, as if she had forgotten he was there. She lifted another spoonful of ice cream to her lips. "I hadn't thought about that until now. I ate a lot after the second one left."

"You did?" Cody held his breath, hoping she would continue. He wanted to know more about her. Why she thought what she did. Why she had never settled down.

"Yeah. And cried a lot too."

"You loved him?"

"I did, but it didn't matter. He left anyway. I never saw him again." Hurt surrounded each of her words.

A boom of thunder and then a flash of lightning filled the air. The lights flickered then went out.

"We're in for a strong storm tonight. Springtime in New England." Cody went looking for the flashlight he kept in a drawer just for these occasions. There was another roll of thunder and then more lightning. "I'll have to check the roof shingles after this one."

He lit one of the candles, setting it on the bar. Even in the shadowy light he could see Stacey's stricken look and pale skin. Her eyes were squeezed closed. At the next flash of lightning they opened wide and held a wild look. She was terrified.

Taking her hand, he led her to the living room, encouraging her to sit on the sofa. He took a seat beside her and pulled her into his chest. Stacey didn't hesitate to bury her face in his shoulder. She shuddered at the next flash of lightning.

For a moment Cody's heart caught. This was what it

should be like all the time. He needed someone he could share his life with, where he could be her safe port in a storm. Could that person be Stacey? Would she let him be that for her?

The flash of lightning, the boom of thunder and rain pelting the house made Stacey jerk and put her arms around Cody. She trembled, her heart pounding. From childhood she'd never been a fan of storms. Too often she been left alone during them. Her mother had forbidden her from coming to her room. Many nights she'd huddled in her bed, trembling with fear. More than once during her travels she'd had to deal with her anxiety over bad weather alone. She curled farther into the security Cody offered.

"Are you okay?" He snuggled her tighter.

The rumble of his deep voice where her ear lay against his chest somehow eased her panic. Would he think she was silly? A grown woman worried over a storm? "I don't like storms."

Lightning flashed again. She shook.

"I've got you. I won't let go."

She felt safe and secure next to Cody. For the first time in her life she could say that. Peeking out the window, she said, "You sure know how to give a girl a show."

He kissed her temple. "I can't take credit for putting this one on but thank you anyway."

Sometime later the lights flickered on again. Stacey slowly pulled away from Cody. "Hey."

"Hi. You better?"

She moved to stand but he held her back. "Yeah. I should go. I've embarrassed myself enough."

"You still look scared and it's still pouring. You're not going anywhere."

"I'll be fine. I've been taking care of myself in worse places and weather for years." She really should get out of Cody's arms. If not, she'd want to stay...too long.

At a distant roll of thunder he gave her a stern look. "Maybe so, but not when I've known about it. You're staying here tonight. You can have my bed."

What was he suggesting? Her eyes widened and she jerked back, shaking her head.

"I'll sleep down here on the couch," he assured her, bringing her back against him once again.

"I can't let you do that."

"Sure you can. You've been helping my girls all afternoon. I think it's the least I can do."

"I'm not sleeping in your bed!" She wanted to make that clear. Fear of the outside kept her there even discussing it.

He raised his hands in a gesture of defeat. "Okay. You can stay down here. I'll get you a blanket and something to sleep in. You know where the bath is. There should be clean towels under the cabinet. For now I'm going to stay right here with you until the storm eases."

"I'd like that." She burrowed closer to him.

Later, when nothing was left but heavy rain, Cody went to his room and returned with one of his T-shirts for her to sleep in, a blanket and a pillow that must have come off his bed. She silently groaned that she would be sleeping on where his head might have been. He dumped his armload on the sofa. "Here you go. I still wish you would take my bed and let me sleep down here."

"I'm good here. Thanks. Goodnight."

Stacey woke to a bang in the kitchen and the smell of bacon. Her intention had been to be gone before Cody woke, but apparently she'd been more tired than she had thought. There was another cling-clang. *What was he doing?*

She had to admit it was nice to wake to the sounds of someone nearby. She'd spent so much time in private housing she rarely awakened to people. There was something soothing about knowing Cody was close. Her eyelids lowered.

A large hand cupped her shoulder and shook her gently. "Stacey, your breakfast is ready."

What? She'd gone to sleep again? Her eyes sprang open. Her gaze lifted to see Cody's smiling face. "Good morning, sleepyhead. Your breakfast is on the table when you're ready."

He left her. She untangled herself from the blanket and followed close behind him.

Cody headed for the kitchen and went around the bar to the stove. There he poured batter on the griddle. She looked at the table and found a plate stacked with perfectly round pancakes, a bottle of syrup and another plate with strips of bacon on it. There was also a pitcher of juice nearby.

"What did I do to deserve this?"

"This is my thank-you for helping with the costumes," Cody announced as he flipped pancakes. He was dressed in a tight T-shirt, well-worn jeans and wore no shoes. She'd never seen a sexier man.

"Haven't you already done that by letting me sleep on your couch?"

Cody looked at her and shrugged. His focus dipped to her chest. Heat shot through her. She'd forgotten she was wearing his thin T-shirt with no bra. Her breasts tingled as her nipples tightened, pushing against the soft fabric.

She turned and headed out of the room but not before she saw the flash of disappointment in Cody's eyes. "Hey, Doc, your pancakes are burning."

Stacey grinned at his uttered oath as she grabbed her clothes from the living room and hurried to the bathroom. She quickly washed her face and used the new toothbrush he'd put out for her last night, put on her clothing and ran her fingers through her hair. Checking the mirror, she saw she'd done the best she could do.

When she returned he asked, "Did you sleep well?" His voice had gone deeper, and held a gravelly note.

"I did."

"You should have been in a bed." His gaze held hers.

She looked at him. Had he wanted to say *my* bed? She tingled low at her center. How would she have responded if he had asked her to sleep with him? He wouldn't have. He wasn't the type of man who would take advantage of a woman when she was scared. They said nothing more for a few seconds, just watched each other.

"Your breakfast is getting cold."

She went to the table and Cody pulled out her chair. "Thank you." When was the last time a male had done that for her? Stacey took her seat. Cody sat. She glanced at him. He was watching her and winked. The flutter in her stomach had nothing to do with hunger.

What would it be like to have breakfast with Cody all the time? To be treated as if she were special? Even her ex-fiancé had never made her feel as important as Cody did. What was she thinking? Cody was just being nice. Her life consisted of living all over the world and his was all about hearth and home.

They finished their breakfast with Cody having a second cup of coffee and her another glass of juice.

"I have to pick up the girls in a few minutes. I can drop you off at your cottage on my way to get them." Cody put his mug down and stood.

"Sounds like a plan."

He began removing dishes from the table. Stacey joined in. When he ran water in the sink she bumped him out of the way with her hip. "You cooked. I'll clean."

He nudged her back with a grin. "My kitchen. You don't get to tell me what to do."

She snatched the dishrag from him.

He reached around her, enclosing her within the circle of his arms. He smelled of man and coffee. She squirmed and his hold tightened, bringing her back against his chest. It was large, firm and secure. His warmth enveloped her. She stilled. For a moment they just stood there. Stacey held her breath.

"Stacey..." He kissed the top of her head.

She turned to face him. Expectant. He leaned into her, pressing her against the counter, making his intention clear. His gaze bored into hers. A flame of desire burned in his before he blinked and it was extinguished. Seconds later she was alone, staggering to remain standing. Cody had stepped around the breakfast bar, putting it between them. "I can't. No matter how much I want to."

Stacey couldn't respond to that. It was no surprise. She'd not been wanted enough before.

"I'll go get some shoes on and take you home," Cody muttered.

Before she knew it, he'd left the room.

On Saturday, nearly a week later, Cody searched the Founder's Day event area for the girls. They had been running from tent to tent excited to finally be attending.

He couldn't help but be pleased with the turnout. It was the largest event of the year and people from the mainland had come over to join in the fun. The vendors ranged from face painters to arts and crafts to local food, all centered on maple syrup. Everyone appeared as if they were enjoying themselves. The committee had planned long and in detail to make the occasion a success. Cody was proud of their efforts.

During the past week he'd had to make a couple of last-minute meetings to handle specifics and issues. In the end every aspect of the weekend was going off smoothly and he hoped it would continue that way through to Sunday evening. The weather had even co-operated by being spectacular.

He couldn't say the same about his relationship with Stacey. She'd been conspicuously absent from his life outside the OR and the daily rounds to see patients. By appearing at the last possible moment then slipping away the second the job was complete, she had curtailed any chance to talk other than on medical-related issues. Cody couldn't blame her. He didn't like knowing he'd hurt her, no matter how justified the reason. What he should say he was well aware of, but what he wanted to say he wasn't so sure of.

That night she'd stayed at his house he'd climbed the stairs alone. All he'd been able to think about had been Stacey in his home and the what-ifs. What if he kissed her? What if she let him cup her breast? What if he asked her to join him in bed? He'd taken a shower. A cold one. Having Stacey so close had played havoc with his libido.

As was his habit, he'd gone downstairs to secure the house for the night and passed the living room. Stacey had been sound asleep. Her fear of the storm must have zapped her adrenaline, taking all her energy. She'd pulled his pillow to her chest and had been under the blanket. He'd had to move on, fighting himself not to wake her and make sure she slept in his bed. With him.

Now he was longing for her. For what could have been. When his pillow had been returned it had smelled of peaches. His T-shirt hadn't fared any better. He'd made more than one move to wash them but couldn't bring himself to do so.

He been doing the right thing by not getting too involved with Stacey. That statement had been on audio repeat all week, echoing inside his head. His mind might understand but his body wasn't agreeing.

He only had to hold out for a little while longer. She would be leaving soon but he missed their talks, even her teasing remarks. More than once he'd tried to convince himself his concerns stemmed from his girls' constant questions about her but he knew better. He wanted Stacey with a driving need that almost overwhelmed him.

She'd been so sassy and happy during their breakfast together last Sunday morning. It hadn't been until he'd touched her that things had started to get out of control. He knew when a woman wanted him and her eyes had said that clearly. For a minute he'd taken advantage of that, almost kissing her but stopped himself. He knew hurt, deep hurt, and wasn't setting himself up for that again. His girls deserved to have someone who wanted them more than anything else. He did too. Stacey had made it clear she couldn't offer them permanency— moving on to the next exciting place was what she wanted more.

It wouldn't have mattered so much if he hadn't recognized there was something extraordinary between them. He couldn't put a name to it but he did know his entire being simmered whenever he was near her. Stacey had to feel it too. Knowing her time there was short didn't change his desire to get to know her better, touch her, kiss her. In fact, it intensified it. At the same time, he needed to protect his girls. He and they were a package deal. Being an adult, he could deal with the void Stacey would create in his life when she left, but he wouldn't put Jean and Lizzy through that kind of loss again.

"Don't the girls need to be getting to the stage soon?" his mother asked.

"We have a few more minutes," he assured her. His parents had arrived the day before.

"Have you thought any more about letting them go with us up to Maine for a few days?" his father asked as they continued along the crowded aisle between the rows of tents.

"You need some time to yourself," his mother commented. "You haven't really let those girls out of your sight in years. It's time to let go a little."

He and his parents had had this discussion more than once in the recent months.

"I'm thinking about it." Cody still wasn't ready to commit to such a big step.

"Stacey!"

The chorus of Jean and Lizzy's voices above the crowd of people jerked his thoughts to where they were. Both girls ran and wrapped their arms around the dark-haired woman who filled his dreams. She wore a pink T-shirt, jeans and tennis shoes. She'd never looked better.

Lizzy and Jean clung to her. It had taken Jean a while

to warm up to Stacey but putting together costumes seemed to have done the trick. Perhaps a little too well.

Stacey hesitated a tad long before she knelt and hugged them in return. As she did she peered over their heads, looking around in alarm. Uncertainty darkened her green eyes as their gazes met. She clearly hadn't planned to run into them.

That moment of uncertainty went against the grain and left him with a bad taste in his mouth. She was dodging them. *Him.*

By the time he reached them, Jean and Lizzy had pulled away and were excitedly telling Stacey about their week and how much Fleur had liked their costumes.

"She said we looked the best!" Jean said to Stacey with hero-worship in her eyes.

Stacey smiled down at her. "I'm glad."

She sounded as if she was.

"Are you ready to dance?" Stacey asked Lizzy.

She nodded. "I know all my steps."

Her joy at seeing the girls appeared genuine. Stacey looked at him again, having to tilt her head back to do so. This time the cloud of anxiety was missing in her eyes. Had it been replaced by hopefulness? He was more conflicted than ever.

"So this is 'super' Stacey," his mother remarked in a congenial tone, stepping around him and extending a hand. "Hi, I'm Cody's mother, Jeanette."

Wearing a stunned expression, Stacey stood and accepted his mother's hand. "Hello. It's nice to meet you." She glanced at him. "Cody didn't tell me you were visiting."

He gave her a pointed look, not caring that his exasperation showed. "You didn't give me chance to."

* * *

Stacey had been skirting him all week so he had her there. Cody had made it clear what he wanted and she would respect that. She wanted the same thing. Separation. Space.

No, she didn't. She wanted him.

For the benefit of both of them they needed distance between them. With a great deal of effort she'd accomplished it but loneliness filled her free time. She hadn't been plagued by that despair in a long time. Since childhood. She'd learned long ago how to be self-sufficient. Depending only on herself for happiness. In a few short weeks she'd backslid into expecting to find happiness with another, but it was a mistake she had been trying to correct and would continue to right. If only she could get her heart to co-operate.

"The girls can talk of little but you," his mother continued with the captivating smile that Cody had inherited.

Stacey wasn't sure how to respond.

Cody clearly took pity on her when he said, "Stacey Ryder, this is my father, Roger Brennan." Cody patted a man on the shoulder who had similar features to him but with silver hair.

She shook Cody's father's offered hand. "It's a pleasure to meet you."

"And you too. I understand you work with my son."

"Yes, sir. I'm Dr. Brennan's clinical nurse, or at least I am for seven more days." A sadness deeper than she'd ever felt settled over her at that thought.

"You *are* going to come see us dance, aren't you?" Jean asked.

Stacey's plan had been to arrive just before the girls were to go on stage, stand in the back long enough to see them dance and then leave without being seen by them or their father. Now all she could do was answer with conviction, "I wouldn't miss it."

Both girls beamed at her.

"It's time we should be getting your costumes on, girls." Cody put a hand on each of their backs, heading them in the other direction. "Fleur said you needed to be dressed and ready to go on time."

His mother put a hand on Cody's arm. "We'll get a seat up front and save you one. Stacey, you will join us?"

It wasn't really a question. Stacey watched Cody and the girls walk away. She was stuck now.

Cody's mother said, "Let's go get those front row seats."

There were no rows of chairs in front of the stage. Instead there were picnic tables. Cody's mother picked out one off to the right of the front of the stage. Mr. and Mrs. Brennan took one side of the table and she sat on the other bench.

"Why don't I go get us all a drink while we wait?" Cody's father asked.

"That sounds wonderful. Thanks, honey." Mrs. Brennan smiled at her husband. She then turned her attention to Stacey. "I understand that you worked nothing less than a miracle with the girls' costumes."

"I wouldn't call it a miracle." Stacey didn't want to carry that responsibility. Why did she feel the sudden need to escape? She'd just been tapping into her creative side.

"That's not how Cody described it."

Stacey smiled. "He only saw it that way because he didn't know how to handle it himself."

Cody's mother's face turned serious. "He's had to be

father and mother for most of the girls' lives. Those more creative touches he sometimes has difficulty with."

"That has to be frustrating for him. He's such a perfectionist with his patients."

"It is. Very frustrating." Her look met Stacey's as if Mrs. Brennan wanted to make sure she clearly understood. "Cody and the girls have survived a very difficult few years."

"He told me."

Mrs. Brennan's eyes went wide, her surprise obvious. "Really? He never talks about Rachael."

"I asked him and he told me."

"Interesting. Because of what happened with Rachael he's always trying to make up for those bad times. He is very overprotective where the girls are concerned. Of himself as well. I wasn't sure I'd ever see the genuine smiles of happiness on Jean and Lizzy's faces like I saw today. It's wonderful. Even Cody has a look in his eyes that I feared was gone forever." Her eyes glistened. "Thank you for that."

Stacey's stomach fluttered with joy, only to turn sour from acute apprehension. She would be leaving soon. Of that there was no doubt. Life seemed unfair to her, to Cody, and even to his girls. It was the wrong place, wrong people and wrong time. She wasn't right for Cody. If they moved past being friends and co-workers there was nothing but pain out there for all of them.

Cody wouldn't keep her. Even if she wanted him to. One day he would push her away. Her father had done it, her stepfather had and then finally so had her fiancé. All the men in her life left her eventually. She wasn't staying around for that to happen again. So there was no reason to start something that had no future. Knowing what it felt like being left behind and the pain it brought, she wouldn't do that to Cody. Or let him do it to her either.

"I don't know if I'm who you should give that credit to. I've not done anything special."

"Maybe just being you is what makes it special." Cody's father approached. Mrs. Brennan added in a low voice, "I'm sure that I've said more than Cody would appreciate." She placed a hand over Stacey's. "Just know that you are special to them."

Stacey fiddled with a loose sliver of wood on the tabletop. When had she last felt special to anyone? Or had someone tell her that she was? It was nice to hear, even if it was coming from Cody's mother.

While they had been talking, people had been settling at the tables around them. It wouldn't be long before the program started. Mr. Brennan joined them and they talked about the island and the festival for a few minutes in between sipping their iced drinks.

Mrs. Brennan's attention moved to somewhere behind Stacey. "I think Cody needs you."

Heat burned her cheeks. What was his mother saying?

She smiled. "I don't mean that, hon, though it might be true. I mean he's waving that he needs you to come to him."

Stacey turned to find Cody standing at the corner of the stage, gesturing for her to join him. She started that way. Once again she was being pulled in despite her vow to remain detached.

There was a desperate note in Cody's voice when she reached him. "I need some assistance with the girls' bonnets. They say I'm not doing it right."

Stacey couldn't help but be pleased. It was nice to feel needed.

"I'll owe you even more than I already do if you could get them on for me."

"I can do that. Where are they?"

Cody took her hand. It was large, solid and secure. Steady. Something about having her hand in his felt right. He pulled her through a gaggle of little girls, around a couple of mothers talking and passed another group of girls to where Jean and Lizzy stood.

"Daddy couldn't do this right," Lizzy said, handing Stacey her bonnet.

She took it from the girl. "To be fair to your father, this does have a degree of difficulty. He doesn't know what I had in mind. Turn around and let me get this on you."

Lizzy turned her back to Stacey.

"Who put your hair in a bun?" Stacey worked at positioning the cap and tying it under Lizzy's chin.

"Daddy."

"He did a nice job on that." She glanced at Cody. He mouthed, "Thank you."

"All done. Okay, Jean, it's your turn."

Jean stepped up and turned her back to Stacey, who soon had the cap secured. "Okay, now let me look at you both."

The girls grinned up at her. "Perfect. Now go dance as good as you look."

Jean grabbed her by the waist and hugged Stacey so tightly she swayed. Cody placed a steadying hand in the small of her back. Trying to ignore the intimate sensation his touch generated, Stacey returned Jean's affection. Lizzy joined them.

"Okay, girls. Let Stacey go. Fleur is trying to get you to come to her."

They took off to where other girls stood dressed in

similar clothing to them. She and Cody walked back to join his parents. This time he didn't take her hand and she missed the contact. Too much.

When they sat down Cody's mother said, "What was the problem?"

"I didn't put their bonnets on like Stacey did."

"I see."

Stacey was afraid she might see too much.

"How did you make those bonnets anyway?" Cody asked.

"I cut the brim off a white hat I had, then cut it in two. That way I had the curve that was needed. Then I used sewing glue on the edges. I hand sewed shoe strings on to tie them with."

"That's impressive." Cody's mother gave her a smile of admiration.

Cody put his hand on her shoulder. "I know. I couldn't have done it without her."

His praise was nice to hear but wasn't making it any easier for her to keep her resolve to remain detached.

The program started and soon the girls and boys were dancing across the stage. Cody sat beside her, close enough that she could feel his warmth. She was so aware of him she had difficulty paying attention to the children in Native American outfits, as English soldiers, and then Pilgrims. He squeezed her hand then let it go when Jean and Lizzy came on stage. They did a beautiful job with their dance.

As soon as the program was over Stacey made a production of checking her watch. For her own good, she needed to leave. "I've got to go."

"Right now?" Cody's disbelief filled his voice.

"I…uh…told Summer that I'd help her with something at two. So I have to go. Please tell the girls for me that they were great."

"I bet they would rather hear that from you." The dark disapproval on Cody's face came close to snuffing out her determination.

"I'm sorry, but I really must go." Why couldn't he leave it alone? She looked at his parents, who were watching her closely, then back to Cody. "It was nice to meet you, Mr. and Mrs. Brennan." She threw those words over her shoulder as she hurried away. She was no longer counting the days but the hours until she could leave the island.

Sunday afternoon, after his parents and the girls had left, Cody made his way to Stacey's cottage. He'd had enough. He had to see her. Put things right between them. Somehow.

He had no intention of bringing anyone disruptive into his world. Stacey was that type of person. The kind that unsettled people. She had certainly had that effect on him. Yet he still couldn't stay away from her.

After Rachael he'd accepted he wasn't a good judge of character. He couldn't make that mistake again. Yet here he was on Stacey's cottage doorstep. Even if there couldn't be anything real between them, he still wanted her. She needed to know that. He had to make the hurt in her eyes go away. She wasn't unaffected by his family. He'd seen Stacey's pride and pleasure in Jean and Lizzy's dancing. Some things she couldn't hide.

He knocked. There was no sound. Knocked again. Was she at the festival? Something made him think she wasn't. Maybe out for a walk? He didn't want to do this at the clinic but if that was the only way, he'd take it. As he turned to leave, the door opened.

"Cody, what are you doing here?" Stacey asked around the door. "Is there an emergency?"

"Of sorts. We need to talk."

"Why?" She pushed at her hair.

"I want to tell you I'm sorry."

She looked away. "You have nothing to be sorry for."

"You're wrong. Do you mind if I come in? Or you could come out here." For a second, he feared she was going to say no to either option. For some reason he needed her to understand how he'd been feeling.

"I'm not really dressed for company."

He could tell she had her hair up on top of her head in a messy arrangement. She wore a long T-shirt and shorts. "I think you look fine." Too fine, really. Even in that outfit he wanted her. He stuffed his hands into his pockets.

"I'll come out." She pushed the door just wide enough for her to exit and stood on the porch.

"Why don't we sit on the steps?" He'd figured this might be hard but had had no idea she'd be so standoffish. Why was he putting this much effort into their relationship or friendship or whatever it was? He'd had enough emotional upheaval in his life without adding more. "Look, on second thoughts, just forget it. I'll leave you alone. I'll see you at work tomorrow." He turned to head down the steps.

She grabbed his arm. "Don't go."

He sank to the porch, his feet on the first step and his elbows on his knees. Stacey sat beside him but not too close. Neither of them said anything for a while.

"I'm sorry I hurt your feelings the other morning." Her slight hiss didn't miss his attention. "I want you to know it isn't about you. It's about me." She shifted beside him, but he didn't look at her. Instead he focused on a knot in the board between his feet.

"What do you mean?"

"Come on. You know exactly what I mean. This thing between us." He waved his hand between them.

Her voice went higher as she said, "There's nothing between us."

Cody sighed but tried again. "Sure there is. I feel it. I know you feel it too. I've seen the way you look at me. How you react when I touch you. The other morning at my house I could see the excitement in your eyes when you thought I was about to kiss you. I know why you are putting up a wall between us. I get it, but I don't like it."

Stacey hopped up and was almost to the door before he could make a move. He stood, preparing to leave. He'd gotten his answer.

"I can't do this," she muttered.

"Do what?" Were they even talking about the same thing?

"I'm not staying on the island. I know you're looking for more than that. I can't give it. It's not fair to you. I won't hurt you or the girls."

"I'm not looking for more than what you can give. What I do know is that I've missed you."

"I've been right—"

He gave her a pleading look. He wanted her to understand. "I mean you being yourself. You making me laugh. You being around. You teasing me."

"I don't do that."

He glared at her. "Yeah, you do."

He took a deep breath, choosing his next words with care. "Look, I like you, Stacey. It's been a long time since I could say that about any woman. And I'm guessing by your actions up until this past week that you liked me too. That alone makes you special. I know we work together and that can complicate things but I want you like I've not wanted anyone in a very long time. Can't we just explore what's between us? Enjoy each other for the time we have left?"

Had he completely lost his mind? Was he that lonely? This was nothing like what he'd promised himself. He'd vowed to protect himself, and his girls, by not getting too involved with the wrong woman. But his vow be damned. He wanted to get to know Stacey better, far better.

He gestured with both hands to emphasize his next words. "I know it's crazy, with you having just a week left, but I can't help myself. I want to spend as much time with you as possible before you leave. Can't we do that?"

Stacey turned to face him, watching him, judging him. She took a step toward him. Her voice was steady with no hint of indecision or hesitation when she said, "I'd like that."

Relief washed through him. "Good. I know this is short notice and I apologize, but the Founder's Day weekend is almost over and I was wondering if you'd like to go with me and get some dinner?"

A slow smile formed on her lips. "That sounds like fun. What about Jean and Lizzy?"

"They left this morning for Maine with their grandparents for a few days. So it'll just be the two of us. Is that okay?" Would she want the buffer of the girls between them?

"More than okay. Give me a few minutes to get dressed."

Cody swung on the porch swing while he waited,

pleased with himself. His powers of persuasion were so refined should he consider going into politics?

Stacey didn't keep him waiting long. Her hair was still up on her head but she wore an exotic-looking dress that he guessed she'd gotten during her travels. It caressed her curves and flowed around her legs. A bright beaded bracelet circled one wrist. Sandals protected her feet and she carried a sweater.

He offered her his hand. She took it. His heart soared. She smiled sweetly. "I'm ready."

CHAPTER SIX

STACEY COULDN'T BELIEVE how quickly she had changed her mind about spending time with Cody. All it had taken was for him to show up at her door and all of her firm resolve had crumbled. It hadn't taken her even a minute to decide she wanted her short time on Maple Island filled with wonderful memories of him. She could have those, and take them to Ethiopia or wherever she went for the rest of her life.

The past week had been miserable. Avoiding Cody outside work had been doubly difficult because her common sense had constantly been at war with her undeniable desire to be with him. She had never felt lonelier in her life. Despite living on a beautiful island during springtime, she wasn't enjoying it. Even the opening celebrations of Founder's Day Weekend had been spoiled because she'd been so wary of running into Cody.

With the air cleared between them it was like they were truly friends. They said little on the ride but there was nothing uncomfortable about the silence. It was as if they were both determined to make the time they had left positive.

The sun shone brightly and the sky was blue as they walked into the festival. She looked forward to really experiencing it. Today she planned to soak it all in. Being with Cody made it even better.

Stacey stopped for a second to tie her sweater around her waist. "Wow, there're a lot of people here today as well."

"With more hours of daylight, people are making the most of the event. It has been a good year. It helps when the weather is nice." Cody looked around with a smile. "There's a band tonight and many folks will stay late for that."

He took her hand but gave her a quick, questioning glance as if asking for permission. Stacey squeezed it, and he gently tightened his grip. As they moved from tent to tent he didn't let go of it. More than one person spoke to him as they strolled along. With each one he introduced her right after returning their greeting.

They were busy looking at handmade weathervanes when someone called, "Cody."

They both looked around to see Dr. Rafael Valdez, who was pushing a stroller, and Summer Ryan coming their way.

Stacey knew them from the clinic. From what she understood, Rafael was a relatively new addition to the staff, only having arrived on the island a few months ago.

"Hi, there." Cody offered his hand and the two men shook.

"You two enjoying the festival?" Summer asked her and Cody.

"Yes, we are." Stacey smiled at Cody, who returned it. She looked into the stroller. "Who do you have with you? I don't believe we've met."

"This is my daughter, Gracie." Pride filled Rafael's voice.

"Hi, there," Stacey said to the girl.

"We're just going for a bite to eat. Want to join us?" Rafael asked.

"Thanks, but we have a few more tents to visit. Maybe another time," Cody said.

"Then we'll see you tomorrow." Rafael waved over his shoulder as he and Summer moved on, Gracie preceding them in her shaded stroller.

Stacey watched them leave. "They make a nice couple."

"Rafael is a topnotch addition to the staff." Cody turned to her. "I hope you don't mind me not accepting their offer. I wanted it to be just us tonight."

Stacey's heart did a pitter-pat. "I like that plan."

They continued walking while looking at the arts and crafts.

He tugged gently on her hand. "I'm getting hungry. How about you?"

"Starving."

Cody steered her toward the food court. "Good. How does a lobster po'boy sound?"

"I don't know. I've never had one."

"It's lobster meat on a bun. I think you'll like it. Willing to give it a try?"

Stacey was confident she would give anything he asked a try. "Sure."

A few minutes later they had their sandwiches and drinks. Luckily, they found an empty table among those set up near the food trucks.

"Goodness, this is so big. I don't know if I can get my mouth around it." Despite what she'd just said, Stacey opened wide, managing it with little trouble.

"Doesn't look like you're having a problem to me." Cody chuckled.

Stacey glared at him. "And to think I thought you had no sense of humor when I first met you."

"Maybe you bring that out in me."

She liked that idea. Cody should smile often. She loved his smile. "I'm glad I can be of some help."

"That's all you've been since you arrived. Help with my patients, help in the OR, help with the girls, and the list could go on."

"You once told me not to put you on a pedestal, I'm going to say the same." She too was afraid she would fall.

"Then we'll agree to be less than perfect." He took another bite of his sandwich.

"That I can certainly agree to."

When they were finished Cody asked, "Would you like to stay and listen to the band or I can offer you the view of the sunset from the point near the lighthouse?"

"I'd love to see the sunset." For the day to start off so depressingly, with her sitting alone in her cottage, it was fast turning into a perfect one.

Hand in hand they walked to his car. Dusk crept in as they rode along the windy road toward the lighthouse. Just before they got there Cody turned off on a smaller road that led toward the beach. Across the water was the Boston Harbor. Lights were blinking on in the buildings.

Cody pulled the car to a stop and turned off the engine. He didn't say anything but took hold of her hand. In silence they watched the play of colors in the western sky. The blend of red, orange and yellow melding into black became the backdrop of their view of Boston.

Stacey had never seen anything more beautiful or been

in a more romantic setting. "Wow, you sure know how to show a girl a good time."

He laughed. "You do have a way with words. Would you like to stay a while longer or for me to take you home?"

"Truthfully?" Could she really tell him what she would like to do?

"Yes."

"I'd like to sit on your porch, look at the stars and listen to the waves."

"That we can do." He sounded pleased with her request. "How about a hot drink to go with the view?"

"Sounds wonderful."

He started the car, turned around and headed up the road. "You know, if we're not careful we'll do everything there is to do on this island on our first date."

"Maybe we can think of something new." She had a few ideas already.

The drive to Cody's wasn't far but he didn't hurry. A light burned over his front door, welcoming them as they entered and walked to the kitchen.

"You go on out and make yourself comfortable. I'll get us something warm to drink." Cody put a kettle on the burner.

Stacey pulled on her sweater before she chose the cushioned settee, sat and slipped off her sandals, tucking her feet under her. Leaning her head back, she closed her eyes and listened to the ocean. Every day should be like this. Since coming to Maple Island, it seemed as if she had stopped running and had started taking time to appreciate the smaller things in life. Many of those Cody had introduced her to.

For years she'd been living six months here, three

months there, and another nine months to a year elsewhere. She'd forgotten what it was like to stay in one
place any length of time. As if she had ever known. Even
as a child she'd moved often. She didn't know how to stay
in one place. This sensation of belonging was surely just
temporary. She would soon get restless and be ready to
move on. Why did she even think she would be happy
settling down?

Soon the kitchen light went out and Cody joined her.
"Don't panic. I turned the lights off so we could see the
stars better."

"I'm not going to panic." After her erratic actions of
late she wasn't surprised he'd believed she might overre-
act. "I wondered if you were trying to be Mr. Romance."

He handed her a mug and took a seat in a chair nearby.

Was he afraid to crowd her? She wanted him close.

"I can be that with or without the lights on." His deep,
rich voice was made more so under the blanket of darkness.

"I like a man with confidence." She enjoyed teasing
him. He was far too serious.

"Did you ever doubt it?"

Stacey could only make out his silhouette but she
clearly heard the inflection in his voice. It mattered to
him what she thought.

"No." She hadn't. How could she? Her body hummed
with excitement whenever he was near. Like now. She felt
the power of his male magnetism continually.

They quietly sipped their drinks. Stacey had never had
a relationship with a man in which she was content to
just share time with him. It was calming. They remained
there while the stars slowly disappeared behind clouds.

"It will rain tonight. But no storm like the other night." Cody's voice came out of the darkness, his hand taking hers and giving it a squeeze.

"It's a good thing the Founder's Day Weekend is over." Her voice sounded soft and relaxed.

"It is." They were talking about nothing significant yet she enjoyed the moment. There was contentment, a feeling of rightness that filled her just being around Cody.

A few minutes went by and the air between them simmered with awareness.

Would he make a move? He'd said he was interested but acted as if he was unsure about asking her for more. Stacey stood, searching for her shoes with her toes. "I'd better go."

"Please don't." There was a note of urgency in the statement as he stood. "Will you stay with me tonight?"

She stepped closer to him. "What took you so long to ask? A girl might think she isn't as irresistible as you led her to believe." She grabbed his shirt, pulled him to her and gave him a kiss she hoped he would remember.

Cody crushed her against him, taking control of the kiss. His lips sauntered across hers as his hands roamed her back before wandering over her cheek to kiss her neck then returning to her mouth. Teasing the seam of her lips with his tongue, he asked for entrance. She gave it and his passion set her on fire. Her hands pulled his head closer as she returned his ardor with a twirl of her tongue. Cody groaned and brought her hips against his, making his desire thickly obvious.

Heat pooled between her legs. Desire had her blood hot and humming. She needed Cody more than anything else in the world.

* * *

Cody had been waiting for an invitation, any invitation, just some indication Stacey wanted to stay. He'd gotten his answer.

He'd purposely chosen to sit in a chair across from the settee to avoid the temptation to pressure her. He enjoyed her company, the peace of just being with her. If that was all she'd offer him then he would accept that. Stacey had brought him back to life. Still, the drive, the desire to touch her had his fingers twitching. There was electricity in the air whenever they were together. Waiting had been agony. He now planned to enjoy every pleasure she offered, for as long as he could.

Stacey's arms circled his neck and she returned his kiss with all the hunger he'd imagined during sleepless nights. His tongue ran along the seam of her lips and she opened like a bloom waiting for sunshine. Her eager greeting turned the kiss into a heated tango.

His pulse pounded in his ears while blood, hot and pulsing, ran to his manhood, making it thick and tall. Her fingers tunneled through his hair in provocative exploration as if she'd been dreaming of touching it. He cradled her butt, pulling her against him. Those curves he'd admired were now in his hands. His fingers traveled up along them until they framed her breasts.

Cody cupped one, lifting it. Full and firm, the only thing wrong with her breasts was that they were still covered. His thumb brushed her nipple and he was rewarded with it standing to sharp attention.

Stacey moaned and wriggled against him.

His length throbbed, begging to have her. If they didn't slow down he would take her on the bare boards of his porch. Stacey deserved better than that. Their first time should be less hectic and far more tender. Reluctantly, he dragged his mouth from hers. "Wooh, woman, you've got me hotter than a firecracker."

She gave him an enticing grin. "I like the sound of that."

Cody let out a low pained chuckle. His mouth gently met hers. Stacey's hands cupped his face and held him there as she deepened the kiss. Her tongue teased his as her hands moved to his shoulders. She kneaded them as she pressed harder against his aching manhood. How like Stacey to let him know exactly what she wanted.

His mouth moved away from hers to leave kisses across her cheek. He stopped to nuzzle the dip behind her ear. She tensed then squirmed, giving him easier access. So she liked that. He flicked the tip of his tongue over the spot he'd just kissed and she quivered.

Stacey, just as he'd suspected, was ultra-responsive. So vitally alive. He'd been dead for too long. This age-old rush of raw desire she sent through him made him feel alive once more. "Like that, do you?"

"I like everything you do to me," she murmured against his temple as her hands ran down his chest to his waist. She pulled his shirt from his pants and slipped her hands beneath. They set his skin on fire as they skimmed across his waist around to his back.

His attention returned to her breasts. He filled his hand with one. Her nipple, pushing against the material of the dress, called to him. He had no intention of disappointing. His mouth covered it. Cody tantalized and teased as Stacey leaned toward him. He had to see her bare flesh, truly touch her.

Giving her another lingering kiss, he whispered, "Let's go upstairs." It was more of a question than a

statement. Cody still wasn't sure she would agree. Stacey had kept him standing on an edge for days now and
she might keep him there. What if she overthought what
they were doing, like he had the other day? It might kill
him to let her go, but he would if that's what she wanted.

"There isn't anything that I'd rather do, but you must
understand that I'm still leaving next Sunday. You know
that, don't you? I won't change my mind."

His chest constricted. He didn't want to think about
that now. "I know. Let's enjoy tonight and worry about
later then."

Her lips met his before she took his hand and pulled
him toward the door. "It just happens I know the way to
your room."

Cody chuckled. "Yes, you do. You didn't seem that
eager to be there last time."

Even in the dim light he could make out her sassy
look. "That was actually the problem last time, I *was*
eager to be there."

Cody pulled her close and gave her a hot kiss that
promised things to come.

On their way through the kitchen he flipped the light
switch off. Stacey tugged on him in her impatience, making him stumble. He couldn't remember a time when a
woman had been this ready for him. His ego soared, as
his heart pounded with excitement against his ribs.

At the stairs, he flipped the light on. Stacey took advantage of the pause to stand on the first step and helped
him remove his sweater. She dropped it and took his hand
again as they climbed further.

She stopped again. This time she kissed him. As she
did so her hands went to his belt, released it and tugged
it free. She let it slip through her hands with a grin and

started up once again. At the top, she confronted him once more. Cody caught her hands. "Two can play this game. It's my turn."

Her eyes narrowed as she teased him with an enticing grin. "You think so?"

His hands went to her shoulders and pushed her sweater off one of them. He placed a kiss on the soft skin he had exposed. It was as smooth as he had dreamed it would be. Stacey shivered. He continued to remove her sweater until her arms were bare. Starting at one shoulder, he kissed down her arm. He continued to love her until he'd sucked each one of her fingers. He then moved his attention to the other side.

As he slowly released her last digit between his lips Cody glanced at Stacey to see that she had her head back, exposing her long neck. Her eyes were closed. Her breasts stood erect while her nipples peaked against her thin dress. She looked like a goddess in the throes of rapture. Kissing the curve of her neck, he promised himself he would make her look like that as often as he could. Her dazed look met his and he grabbed her hand, leading her into his bedroom. Enough of that game.

In his bedroom, he left her alone beside the bed long enough to turn on the lamp on his desk. Stacey stood watching him with hooded eyes. He returned to her, bringing her into his arms and giving her a tender kiss as his fingertips lightly brushed the backs of her arms. She trembled. He'd never had a woman respond so profoundly to his touch.

Her hands moved to the buttons of his shirt. She made slow, tantalizing work of removing a button from its hole. Her fingers were like the best-quality down as they traveled over the skin of his chest again and again. With each touch his manhood jerked. He watched her movements, the efficacy of her fingers and their length, despite her small hand. Even that simple action on her part filled him with awe.

When the last button came undone she pushed his shirt wider over his chest and studied him with a small smile. The palms of her hands came to rest on his pectorals. She teased the hair there, before she leaned in and placed her lips over his heart.

He pulled her face up and captured her mouth, unable to resist kissing her. His hands went to her hips and he gathered her dress up until he found her silken panties. Cupping her bottom, he squeezed gently, bringing her against his hard, hot length. Could anything be more perfect than the feel of Stacey against him?

Finding the bottom edge of her panties, he slowly traced it around to the crevice of her legs. Slipping the tip of a finger under the elastic band, he brushed it over her skin, moving inexorably toward her center.

Stacey trembled. He loved drawing a reaction from her. Widening her stance a fraction, she offered him access. Unable to resist, he ran his finger over her mound, then slowly slipped between her folds. She stilled, as if anticipating his next move. Cody had no intention of disappointing. He tightened his hold at her waist before his finger entered to find her center wet and waiting.

Instantly Stacey released a held breath and pressed into his hand, moaning. He pulled away. She groaned in complaint.

"Panties have to go." He pulled them down to her knees. She kicked them off and he raised her dress again. He didn't hesitate to cup her center. Stacey squirmed. Cody's finger entered her again. Her hands gripped his shoulders while her head fell back as his finger pushed and pulled, teased and titillated her. Her gaze found his, held. Stacey's green eyes were wide and misty with pleasure. His chest tightened with pride. Soon she shattered, and shivered, having found intense satisfaction.

He held her as she leaned against him.

"My, Doctor, you have magical hands," she muttered against his chest.

He chuckled low in his throat. "Thank you, but I have other parts that are just as magical. You haven't seen anything yet."

Stacey, still weak in the knees and holding on to that feeling of floating away, pulled back and met his gaze. "Promises, promises."

Cody swept her off her feet and dropped her on the bed with a bounce. "That sassy mouth is going to get you into trouble one day. You'd better be careful who you tease."

She grinned. This Cody she could learn to love. No. She wouldn't let that happen.

He'd pulled her dress from beneath her and continued until he had it off over her head.

Standing above her, he studied her. She lay bare to him except for her bra and sandals.

Bringing a foot up, she unbuckled her shoe. Simmering desire sparkled in his dark eyes. It flared the glowing embers low inside her into roaring flames that only he could extinguish. She dropped the shoe to the floor and started on the other.

Cody's look flickered to what she was doing then slowly traveled over her. "You are so sexy. Even more so than I dreamed."

He'd been dreaming about her? Shoe discarded, her fingers moved to the clasp of her bra between her breasts.

"Don't. Let me." He came down on one knee beside her. With a nimble flip he had her bra opened.

At the hiss of his inhaled breath her body went on full alert. Did he actually like what he saw? She dismissed that insecurity when he cupped her naked breast, weighing and caressing it as if it was precious.

"Perfect," he breathed, before his lips claimed her nipple.

Stacey involuntarily arched, offering him all.

Cody's tongue tugged, curled and enticed her nipple until her core became a tight fist of need. After a soft blow across her damp skin that only made it more sensitive, he moved to the other breast and cherished it in turn.

Stacey feared she couldn't take much more. A craving burned in her like a live thing.

Cody's lips found hers as his hands explored her body. She pushed at his shirt until there was nothing between them. They touched chest to chest, heated skin to heated skin. Breaking off the kiss, Cody came to a half-seated position and jerked his shirt the rest of the way off. When he returned to her, Stacey's hand went to the front of his pants and caressed his solid ridge.

The hot length of him bulged against his zipper. She freed the button from its hole. She had to touch all of his strength. Pushing at his pants, she murmured, "These have to go."

He rolled away and kicked off his loafers. While he did that she untangled her arms from her bra. Standing with his back to her, Cody dropped his pants.

She'd never thought of herself as being a woman who admired a man's backside but Cody's was worth admiration. Rounded and firm, it was a perfect specimen above his thick muscled thighs. His was the type that could fill pants or hands just right. He turned, and she gasped. He was all glorious, gorgeous and generous male. Knowing he was hers for the night enhanced his masculine beauty.

Stacey offered her hand. He took it and she drew him to her. He slowly sank over her until he completely covered her. His mouth found hers for a tender kiss that hinted at barely held restraint.

Cody pulled back and looked at her, his fingers stroking her cheek. "You are the most amazing person I know."

His words flowed soft and sweet as water over rocks in a stream. Helplessly spellbound by his possessive gaze, she felt as though for once she stood out in a crowd. No one had ever said anything like that to her. She would cherish those words forever. She'd always dreamed of being special to someone.

"I want you so bad I hurt with it," Cody groaned.

She slid her hand around the nape of his neck and brought his lips to hers. Nipping the bottom one, she licked the spot soothingly. "I want you too."

With a quick movement he rolled away from her. He opened his bedside table drawer, pulled out a small foil package and opened it. Seconds later he was covered and he returned to her. His hands tightened on her waist. He gave her a kiss that started out gentle until he increased the pressure. Meanwhile, his hand skimmed over her hip, following the line of her body to her thigh. He shifted to the side, his hard length pressed against her.

Blood roared in her ears. She kneaded the muscles of his back with an impatience that made her breaths uneven. He ran his lips along the seam of her mouth with the tip of his tongue as his fingers tangled in her curls.

She opened her mouth in welcome as did her legs. Every fiber of her femininity silently begged him to join her.

Cody adjusted once more, bringing the tip of his manhood to her center. He nudged her begging heat but held in place. She flexed toward him.

"Shh." He softly kissed her as his palm brushed her nipple. "Easy. We have all night." He prodded her entrance.

She couldn't bear it. Every nerve in her body was tight with anticipation. Stacey squeezed her eyes shut in order not to beg. Need twisted and throbbed within her.

"Stacey." Her name was a barely audible whisper coming from deep within him. "Open your eyes. I want you to know it's me here with you."

"Like I could ever forget," she moaned, but she opened her eyes.

His intense gaze held hers without blinking as he deliberately, inch by precious slow inch, sheathed himself inside her to the hilt. He'd done it so gradually she feared she might die before he found home. Cody paused as if savoring the moment, her.

No one had ever done that before. Others had been so quick that the act had been far more about them than her. Even her ex-fiancé hadn't taken the time or made the effort to really make love to her. That should have been her first sign he hadn't been right for her. There was more than sexual passion between her and Cody. They were making an emotional connection. That realization both excited and disturbed her.

He leisurely arched his hips, pulling away until he almost left her before returning in the same excruciating motion. Stacey wanted to scream, *Go faster!* but at the same time his actions were so sweet she never wanted them to end. All the while Cody watched her, his dark eyes almost bottomless. His skin was drawn tight across his cheeks as if it took enormous effort to control himself.

She ran her hands over his chest, shoulders and arms, testing and memorizing the texture of his skin and the muscle mass beneath it. Still he eased in and out of her, making her wiggle with frustration when she feared he might leave her. She bit her bottom lip as the knot of burning need grew. Lifting her hips, she silently pleaded for…what she wasn't sure.

Cody's lips found hers as the tangle of need and want contracted. He increased the pace. She joined him, encouraging him. They participated in a game that was theirs alone. The knot at her center grew, expanded and throbbed. Grasping him, her fingers raked his skin. She cried for him to stop then begged for him to continue. Finally, the twisted white-hot need gave way. Quaking, she soared into heavenly oblivion, keening Cody's name.

He remained deep within her while she drifted back to reality. He kissed her on the forehead before he stirred again. He soon shifted into a driving rhythm. Confident she didn't have it in her to catch up and match his pace, Stacey surprised herself. Wrapping her legs around Cody's waist, she pulled him to her. In a frantic final shove, Cody groaned his pleasure long and low.

He fell away from her. One of his hands remained at her waist and a leg was still thrown over hers.

Cody wasn't new to lovemaking. For heaven's sake, he'd been married, but he had never experienced anything as soul shaking as what he'd just shared with Stacey. He'd poured everything in him into the act and been rewarded with Stacey's ego-affirming response. Would he live through another joining? And there would be another.

When his breathing finally evened out, he rolled to his side, propped his head on an elbow and smiled down at her. He received a grin in return as she caressed his chest.

"It's nice to know you keep your promises." A finger-tip followed the line of his hair going south.

"I told you not to doubt me."

"That you did." Her hand drifted lower.

Cody placed one of his over hers. "Don't be teasing me. I'm not as young as I once was. You'll have to give me a few minutes to recuperate."

Stacey pushed his shoulders to the bed and straddled him. Her lips wore a devious smile. "What if I do all the work?"

CHAPTER SEVEN

STACEY WOKE TO the gray light of day. Rain lightly tapped against Cody's large bedroom window and the sound of waves crashing were a faint reminder the ocean was near.

"Good morning." Cody's deep raspy sleep-laden voice sent a ripple of desire through her. Could she ever get enough of him?

She turned so she could see his face and smiled. "Good morning to you too." It seemed as if it had come quickly. After their night together she was exhausted, while at the same time invigorated. Her nerves still quivered with awareness of the sexy man beside her.

Cody shifted so that her head rested in the hollow of his shoulder. They were quiet. She watched the rain. When she'd come to Maple Island she would never have thought a morning like this was possible. She'd never felt more complete than when she was with Cody, but that would be over soon. Too soon. Mentally shaking her head, Stacey pushed that thought away. She refused to let anything ruin this moment.

She moved until she was lying over Cody's chest. She cupped his sexy stubbled cheek and kissed him tenderly. "Thanks for last night." She grinned. "The middle of the night and early this morning."

"My pleasure. Anytime." His kiss wasn't the frenzied type of the night before; instead it was passionate, as if he wanted to tell her something he couldn't voice.

They both drifted off to sleep again in each other's arms.

The next time Stacey woke it was to Cody fondling her breast. Instantly desire shot through her. It was still gloomy outside but warm and cozy next to Cody.

He rolled over her, his lips finding hers. "Mmm...this is a nice way to start a day."

She brushed a finger along his extended manhood.

"Woman, you're going to kill me."

Sometime later they made their way to the bathroom for a shower. It turned into a long one, with her washing him then him her. Before they knew it the water had turned cold.

Stacey kissed his chest as they dried each other off. "We'd better get going or we're going to be late for work. My boss is a demanding one."

Cody grabbed her butt and pulled her against him, giving her a deep erotic kiss. "You bet he is, but why don't you ask him if you can come in late today?"

One thing she had learned about Cody was that he was super-dedicated to his job. He was never late and didn't miss any time. She looked at him with disbelief. "You actually want to play hooky for a few hours?"

"I do. I don't have any surgery scheduled this morning and only paperwork to look forward to. I thought maybe we could have a leisurely breakfast here or at the bakery."

Stacey looked at him askance. "So what you're saying is that spending time with me is preferable to doing paperwork?"

He stopped her hand from toweling off his chest and

looked at her. "Something like that. But the real truth is that I just want more time with you."

"What's happened to the Cody I know?"

"Possibly you." His words whispered across her shoulder as he turned her and dried her back.

That sounded too close to caring for her comfort. She needed to get things back to a lighter note. "I'd rather stay here and eat."

Cody stood confidently in front of her in all his male glory and said, "Pancakes or bacon and eggs?"

She was tempted to take him back to bed. Her addiction to Cody Brennan must be cured. It wasn't healthy. "Bacon and eggs."

Pulling her against his warm naked body, he said, "Sounds almost as tasty as you." He nibbled at her neck.

She broke the embrace. "I'm hungry."

"Me too." He gave her a wolfish grin.

"None of that until you have fed me." She'd brought his shirt into the bathroom with her. Pulling it on, she buttoned it and rolled up the sleeves.

"Mmm... I don't know if I can keep my attention on frying bacon with you dressed like that."

"You know, I could just make it into an apron." Giving him a wicked expression, her hands went to a button.

He groaned. "As much as I appreciate the possibilities...but I promised you food."

She brushed her fingertips across his chest on the way out of the door. "And I want you at full strength."

Cody joined her in the bedroom dressed in just jeans and nothing else. She was going to have a hard time keeping her hands off him. If she wasn't careful, things would get out of hand. Still, she couldn't bring herself to leave. She wanted all of Cody she could get in the time remaining to them.

They went downstairs, picking up their discarded clothing as they went. She hung hers on the newel post and Cody placed his on top of hers.

"While I fry the bacon, would you butter toast and beat the eggs?"

"Sure."

A little while later she was busy with a bowl and whisk when Cody came to stand behind her. "Where did you learn to beat eggs?"

"I'm not really very good in the kitchen. My mom always ate out or bought in food. There was a cafeteria in college, and at the hospitals. When I went to work there were always cooks to see to the crew's meals. So I never had a need to learn."

"Then let me give you your first lesson." He wrapped his arms around her. The heat of his chest warmed her back. Cody placed his hands over hers. He then tilted the bowl slightly and briskly whipped the eggs.

She rubbed her butt against him. "I think I would be a good cook if all my lessons were given like this."

Cody chuckled. It vibrated all the way up her spine.

"Is there anything you're not good at, Doctor?"

"There are a few things, I assure you." There was a note in his voice that made her suspect he referred to his past. Would he ever let what had happened go?

As far as she was concerned, he was just about perfect. Her heart squeezed. She would miss him when she was gone. Unwilling to let anything harm their beautiful morning together, she turned and put her arms around his waist, laying her cheek on his chest. "You couldn't convince me of that."

"Something wrong?" Cody sounded concerned, the eggs forgotten.

"No, I just needed a hug."

He squeezed her tight for a second then released her. "I'd better get these eggs on."

Stacey moved to stand close to him, leaning against the counter. "Did your mother teach you to cook?"

"No, I learned out of necessity. Taking two young children out to dinner every night turned out to be a bigger fiasco than me trying to prepare a meal. Plus I didn't want to raise them on fast food."

Like she had been.

"I was determined to learn how to make at least a few solid meals. I still have disasters every now and then, but basically I can put together a nutritious meal in a fairly short time."

"Once again you're an amazing man. Everyone should be so lucky to have you as a daddy." Cody was the type of father she wished she'd had. This morning would be one of those precious memories she would take with her when she left.

It was around noon when there was a knock on Cody's clinic office door. He called, "Come in.

Stacey strolled in with a smile on her face. He liked that look much better than the one that had been there the entire week before. His preference really was the expression of bliss Stacey had when she found her pleasure beneath him.

"Hey, I wanted to talk to you about the senator's son, if you have a few minutes."

"I always have a minute for you." Even to his own ears he sounded like Alex when Maggie was around. Surely he wasn't that lovesick. *Love?* He and Stacey had both agreed in not so many words that emotions weren't part of their arrangement. If they weren't, he was afraid he'd taken a large step over the line. She'd made it clear she wouldn't be staying for any reason.

"That's nice to hear." She started around the desk.

"Stop right there."

She jerked to a stop. Her brows rose and she gave him a questioning look.

"I just want to make it clear before we start talking that I'm going to stay over here, keeping this desk between us, because I don't think I can get through the conversation otherwise."

Stacey gave him a wicked grin. "Got the hots for me, do ya?"

"Yeah, that would be an understatement." He was already thinking about having her again. About kissing that spot behind her neck that made her squirm.

She didn't blink when she said, "Sounds good to me."

Would she ever stop surprising him?

Taking one of the chairs in front of his desk, she crossed her legs and gave him a self-satisfied smile. "No comeback, Doc?"

He had one but it wasn't something he should be doing at the clinic in the middle of the day. "You'd better watch that mouth. I keep telling you it's going to get you into trouble."

Her voice went low and seductive. "What kind of punishment did you have in mind?"

He gripped the edge of the desk to keep himself from hurling himself over it and grabbing her. "You come to my place tonight for dinner and I'll show you."

"Will I be expected to participate?" Stacey leisurely swung her foot. She was enjoying this.

"Oh, you can count on that."

"Then I wouldn't miss it. What time?"

"Seven?" He needed time to do some special grocery shopping.

Stacey nodded. "I can't wait." Then she actually winked at him.

When was the last time he'd traded bedroom talk with a woman? And not in the bedroom. He'd never done so. What was happening to him?

She straightened in her seat and her look turned serious. "I think Salty is getting the best out of the senator's son. He's doing all of his therapy without complaint now."

"I hear a *but* coming."

Stacey's lips pursed and she nodded. "He's still seriously grappling with the idea of a limp for the rest of his life. I'm worried about his emotional stability more than anything."

"I'll have Rick look in on him. He worked wonders with Fleur. Maybe it'll work again."

Stacey stood. "Then I guess that's it. I've got a hot date to get ready for so I'll see you later." She gave him a grin and a little wave over her shoulder on the way out.

A few hours later Cody was putting the final touches on the small table on the porch where he planned they would eat their meal. His romance skills were so rusty he was nervous about the evening.

The doorbell rang. She was here. He hurried to the door.

Stacey stood on the stoop looking adorable. Her hair was down and swung freely around her shoulders. The slight breeze lifted a few strands and blew them across her face. She brushed them away. The simple but feminine dress she wore fit tightly to her body then flared out around her hips. It was a short one this time that showed an amazing amount of her breathtaking legs. A pair of almost-not-there sandals were on her feet. Her smile gave her both a vivacious and beautiful appearance. He was completely captivated.

Cody pulled her inside and took a deep inhalation of her peach scent before he kicked the door closed. He kissed her with all the pent-up passion he'd been tamping down all day. Her arms came around his neck and she leaned into him. When they broke apart they were both breathing heavily.

A buzzing came from the kitchen. He released her and hurried down the hall. "I have something in the oven."

She followed. "You'd better not burn my supper."

He pulled the hot pot out of the oven.

"It smells wonderful." She was the one who smelled like heaven. He had to get a grip on himself or he'd be groveling at her feet.

"What do we have there?" She tried to look in the pot when he removed the top.

"Brennan pot roast."

Pursing her lips, she nodded. "I feel important. Not just pot roast but Brennan pot roast."

"Are you making fun of the cook?"

"I'd never make fun of someone feeding me." She smiled amiably at him.

He gave her a narrow-eyed gaze. "Good, because you'd have to watch me eat and do without if you had been. Why don't you go on out on the porch while I finish up here? We're going to eat out there."

"You don't need my help?"

"I've got it. I'll be out in a minute." He stirred the beans in the pot on the stove. When he went to join her she was standing at the rail, looking out at the ocean as if she was contemplating a puzzling problem. He placed their plated meals on the table.

She turned to him. "This looks amazing."

He held her chair for her.

"The girls would love to see you now." She sat.

"I can hear them giggling. They're not used to their father romancing a woman."

"Are you romancing me?" She studied him as if she couldn't believe herself worthy of his actions.

"I like to think so. That was the plan." He took his seat across from her.

Their meal was slow and easy. They talked of movies they had seen, places they had been and their favorite meals. Cody enjoyed every minute of it. Stacey was intelligent and engaging, in his eyes the perfect dinner guest.

Stacey placed her fork on her plate. "Uh... I've been thinking."

His chest constricted. About what? "I'm not sure I like the sound of that."

"I'd like to take a walk on the beach."

Relief eased the tension in his shoulders. He had been afraid she might want to call a halt to their relationship.

"Then come back and show you just how sexy I think you are."

His manhood immediately sprang to life. He could forgo the walk for the latter but he would go along with her plans. Anything to keep her in his arms and bed for as long as possible.

* * *

The last few days and nights had been the most amazing, exhilarating and fascinating Cody had ever known. Stacey was everything he'd ever dreamed of in a woman. She was as exciting and entertaining in bed as out.

They worked side by side during the day, exchanging small smiles when nobody was watching. In the evening they had dinner and then sat on the porch until after dark. Hand in hand they would climb the stairs to his bedroom. Stacey satisfied all his desires and more. She continued to surprise him. Aggressive and demanding at times, she could be just as tender and giving at others.

Today those days and nights of heated pleasure would end. His mother and father were bringing the girls home. He expected them at any moment. Their return was bittersweet. He had missed his girls but tonight he would miss Stacey too. His heart was made even heavier by the fact that in just three days Stacey would be gone for good.

Their lovemaking the night before had been slow, deliberate and utterly poignant. Stacey seemed as aware their time together was nearly over as he was. A sick feeling filled his gut. He had to start adjusting, accepting it must end. Now he was waiting at the ferry for his family to arrive. So why did it feel like part of it was still missing? That idea he refused to examine. It would get him nowhere.

He hadn't asked Stacey to come along, believing them being together to meet the girls might send them the wrong message. Before he'd left the clinic he had told her he was leaving to meet the ferry. She smiled but it didn't reach her eyes and she said, "I'll see to things here."

He watched as the ferry pulled into port, the ramp came down and cars started to unload. Soon he saw Jean and Lizzy waving excitedly at him. He returned the greeting, spying his parents behind them. The second the girls were off the ferry they ran to him, wrapping their arms around him.

"Hey, Daddy. We missed you," they each said to him.

"I missed you too," Cody said. He had, yet he was confident that the separation had been good for all of them. He had needed to let go temporarily.

"We had the best time." Jean beamed up at him.

He went down on one knee and wrapped them in his arms. "I want to hear all about it." A few minutes later, after he had spoken to his mom and dad, he herded them all off to his car.

Lizzie said, "We brought something home for Stacey."

His chest ached. "You did?"

Excitement filled Jean's voice as she said, "We got her a bracelet to replace the one she gave me. Now she can remember me when she leaves."

"I'm sure Stacey will like that." He had no doubt she would.

"Can we call her? Go see her?" Lizzy asked.

He drove out of the parking lot. "We'll get in touch with her soon. Right now we need to get you home. So, Mom and Dad, how was your trip?"

Stacey tried to push away her feelings of being left out. She didn't belong with Cody when he met his family. She wasn't a member of that group. She understood that in her mind but her heart tugged her to the harbor. Knowledge didn't make her heart hurt any less. She'd known she was getting in over her head, had tried to stop it, but couldn't. Cody's magnetic pull was just too strong. She and Cody hadn't discussed the fact she would be returning to her cottage that night instead of being in his bed. They both knew the score.

Going home to an empty cottage held no appeal so she worked late. Stacey updated all the patient charts and had done some work that wasn't necessary until the next week. She even made a second round to check on the patients. She didn't want Cody to have to come in for an emergency on the first night of the girls' return or while his parents were visiting. At least, that was the excuse she used.

Instead of going home, she chose to go to Sunbeam Victuals and Delectables for a cup of hot tea and a vegan sandwich. Not her favorite fare but a change from Cody's high-calorie meals. There she wouldn't have to worry about running into him.

The last few days had been the most contented of Stacey's life. She and Cody worked together during the day occasionally sneaking a kiss when no one was around. In the evenings she went to his house. Sometimes she helped him prepare dinner and other times she sat and talked to him while he worked. They most often talked about his childhood which was almost idyllic compared to hers. Sometimes she would share one of her experiences in a different country.

She'd never before shared this type of connection with another human being. Cody hadn't only become her lover but her friend. Those were more difficult to find. She'd always looked forward to leaving one post and been excited about the next but this time she was dreading the change.

She was climbing into her car when her cellphone rang. To her surprise the phone ID told her it was Cody. "Hi."

"Could you come over?" He sounded as if he wasn't

sure about asking or was afraid she might refuse. Still, her heart skipped a beat.

"Aren't the girls there?"

"Yes, they're the ones who asked me to call."

It hurt that it wasn't him who'd wanted to call. Even though she felt compelled to go, it wouldn't help her start detaching herself from Cody. It had been years since she'd let someone get so close to her. "I don't know. I'm tired. I'm just heading home." She had been up most of the night with him so it was a sweet tired.

"Just for a minute." His flat tone implied he was uncomfortable about insisting.

"I don't think it's a good idea." She was confident it wasn't. It would only make it harder for her. Possibly them.

His voice lowered. "The girls brought you a surprise or I wouldn't insist."

She couldn't not go now. Everything in her wanted to see Cody anyway. If just for a moment. She sighed. "Cody."

"We're adults. We can do this." He sounded as unconvinced as she felt. "The girls are refusing to go to bed and it's a school night."

He was laying the bricks of guilt on her.

"My mother and father are here also. They would like to say bye before they leave."

"They don't really know me." Her being friends with his parents was just one more level of involvement she didn't need.

"They feel like they do after they've spent a few days with the girls. I understand you were the topic of conversation for most of the trip. You make an impression on people." His voice dipped lower. "You sure have on me."

Warmth poured over her. He had on her as well. "Okay, but I'm only staying for a few minutes. I'm just leaving Phoenix's now."

"Thanks for doing this."

The pathetic thing was she wasn't even fooling herself. Everything in her drew her to Cody.

When she pulled up to Cody's house the porch light was on. What would it be like to come home all the time to someone who cared enough to leave a light burning for you? She tapped lightly on the door and it was immediately opened.

Jean and Lizzy said in unison, "Stacey!" They wrapped their arms around her waist for a hug. She returned their embraces. Her heart swelled. She could learn to love this type of reception.

"We watched the fishing boats come in, hiked to a waterfall and went to the national park," Jean said, so fast Stacey almost missed some of it.

She smiled. "It sounds like you had a wonderful time." Stacey glanced up to see Cody standing in the hall. Longing filled his eyes. Did he see it in hers as well?

"Girls, let Stacey come in," he said gruffly.

They let go of her and scurried down the hall into the living room. Stacey closed the door behind her and followed them. As she passed him, Cody took her hand, raised it to his lips and placed a kiss in her palm. His gaze held hers. Stacey quaked. A hot response pooled at her center. Just as quickly he released her. They continued down the hall. His parents stood when she entered.

Mrs. Brennan said, "Hello again."

"Hi. Did you have a good trip?"

She nodded, giving Stacey a studying look. "We did. Maine is beautiful."

Did his mother see what was between her and Cody? "It is. I worked in a hospital there for a month. Hello, Mr. Brennan."

He smiled at her. "Nice to see you again, Stacey."

"We brought you something," Jean announced, holding out a box.

Lizzy snatched it from her hand. "I wanted to give it to her!"

"Let's be nice, Lizzy." Stacey stopped herself and her eyes jerked to where Cody stood in the doorway. She'd just disciplined his child in front of him.

"Stacey's right, that wasn't very nice, Lizzy," Cody said in a calm tone.

Jean said, "You can give it to her."

"That's nice of you, Jean," Stacey praised her. "May I see what's in the box?"

"It's something so you will remember us," Jean stated.

That wouldn't be a problem for Stacey. The reverse, in fact. She took the box, removed the top and inside found a multicolored stone bracelet. "It's beautiful."

"Now wherever you go you'll think of us." Lizzy looked at her eagerly.

"Thank you so much." Stacey slipped it on her wrist and placed the box on the coffee table. She then went down on one knee and opened her arms wide. The girls stepped into her embrace for a hug. "I love it. Thank you for thinking of me. You have my promise I'll always think of you both when I wear it." She looked over their heads at Cody and blinked to keep the moisture in her eyes from spilling over. This was just the type of emotional upheaval she'd been guarding herself against.

"Okay, girls, it's time for you to get ready for bed. You

have school tomorrow." Cody placed a hand on each of the girls' shoulders.

Stacey let them go. "Better do what your daddy says."

The girls went first to one then the other of their grandparents and told them goodnight before they left the room.

"I'll be up in a few minutes to tuck you in," Cody called from behind them.

Stacey stood then shifted from one foot to the other, unsure what to do next. "Uh…it's time for me to get going as well. I've had a long day. I understand you're leaving tomorrow." She spoke to Cody's parents.

"We are. We're taking the earliest ferry off the island," Cody's mother said.

"Then I'll say goodbye now. It has been nice to meet you. I wish you a safe trip home."

Mrs. Brennan gave her a thoughtful look. She acted as if she wanted to say more but stopped herself. "It's been nice to meet you too."

Mr. Brennan nodded and smiled.

"I'm going to walk Stacey out," Cody said to no one in particular.

Stacey started toward the door with Cody close behind. She stepped outside and Cody came with her, flipping off the porch light and closing the door behind him. He pulled her into his arms. His lips joined hers in a sizzling kiss that slowed to a tender one. He continued to hold her close as he nuzzled her neck. "I'm going to miss you tonight."

This wasn't making it any less stressful on either of them. She put her hands on his chest and stepped back. "I have to go. See you tomorrow."

This was painful on a level she'd not experienced before. Grateful that the darkness hid her tears, she made her way to the car. Half an hour later she pulled a pillow to her and curled around it, hoping she could get at least a few hours' sleep.

CHAPTER EIGHT

Leaving Cody's house had to have been the most difficult thing she'd ever done. Every fiber in her being had
wanted to stay. Had wanted him, wanted them, but more
than that wanted to have a place where she belonged.

Family had been something she had grown up wishing
for. Being a member of a loving group that cared about
each other, no matter what. At one time she'd thought
that would be a reality of hers but not now. She'd lost
that dream. Still, it pulled at her at times, like the scene
she had just been a part of at Cody's.

She had it bad. Had jumped over the line. This was
just what she had fought against. Since her fiasco with
her ex-fiancé she'd managed to remain unattached to
anybody. Not this time. But she understood the score.
Cody wanted someone who would stay on Maple Island,
be there for him and his girls. Or did he really? Anyway,
that wasn't something she was capable of doing. What if
she screwed it all up and he left her?

All she knew was to keep moving. It was safe. Her
visit on Maple Island had proved what staying in one
place too long did to a person. She'd become attached to
him and the girls, and would carry the pain of leaving

them with her forever. It was a hurt she'd said she would never let herself bear again. And yet...

Even if Cody asked her to stay, she couldn't. But he wouldn't ask. He wouldn't let go of his fear that the marriage he wanted wasn't possible. He'd been hurt too deeply before. She wouldn't take the chance she might fail him. Cody had already suffered through one demoralizing marriage. She couldn't do it to him again. He deserved better.

Determined they would remain friends and on good terms, she would square her shoulders and find the fortitude to focus on work until it was time for her to leave. After all, nothing had really changed except they had stopped sharing a bed. But that was the change she hated most.

Despite two sleepless nights from being without Cody, she decided when Saturday morning arrived sunny and warm she would go to Boston and do some sightseeing. She took the midmorning ferry. She'd not seen any of the city except for the inside of a hospital. Today she would play tourist, for tomorrow she would be gone.

Refusing to dwell on the turn her life had taken, she put all her efforts into walking the Freedom Trail. She followed the painted directions on the street leading to all the important historical buildings that had been built before America had gained its independence. She saw the site of the Boston Tea Party, went inside Faneuil Hall to explore it, listening to the ghosts of the American Forefathers debating declaring independence from Great Britain. She stopped in the bustling market for lunch before returning to her walk that ended at the North Church that had been an integral part of Paul Revere's night ride. She even took time to climb through the tall ship the *USS*

Constitution, which she'd seen from the air when she and
Cody had flown to the hospital. She made it a full day.

The only thing that marred her visit was the occasional
thought slipping into her head that Cody would like this
or she wished the girls could share that. The one conces-
sion she made to missing Cody's family was buying Jean
and Lizzy a copy of *Make Way for Ducklings* at the Old
Corner Bookstore. She couldn't help herself. The classic
tale of the mallard ducks taking a stroll in the park was
one she was confident the girls would enjoy.

With time on her hands and the next ferry still a few
hours off, she decided to go to an afternoon movie. It
would be months before she would have a chance to see
a new release again. Ethiopia was a long way from home.
From Maple Island. From the clinic. The girls. Cody.

She'd been back at the cottage long enough to shower
and pull on one of Cody's T-shirts that she'd brought
home with her when there was a pounding on her door.
She pushed the curtain to one side. Cody stood on her
porch. Concern filled his face. His hand rose as if he was
going to knock again.

When she opened the door he stepped in and grabbed
her, lifting her off her feet. It was heavenly being held by
him again. His words rushed out, his worry surround-
ing each of them. "I've been trying to get in touch with
you all day."

"Is something wrong?" She searched his face. Her
heart raced from just being so close to him. She would
miss him every day for the rest of her life.

"No. I just couldn't find you. I've been calling you
for hours. I thought you might have left without telling
me goodbye. Why haven't you answered your phone?"

"I turned the volume down when I went into the movie and I forgot to turn it back up. I would never leave without saying something to you." She knew too well how it felt when someone you cared about just disappeared without warning.

Cody set her on her feet but didn't let her go, his gaze meeting hers penetratingly. "Movie? Where have you been?"

She wasn't used to someone keeping tabs on her. "I went to Boston for the day."

Disbelief covered his face. "Alone?"

"Yes." Before coming to Maple Island she'd done everything by herself. She'd not checked in with anyone in years. No one had cared enough about her to ask her to do so.

"I wanted to invite you to lunch. But I couldn't find you and kept calling. I got worried. I even lied for the first time in my professional life and said I had an emergency so that someone from the day-care center could come stay at the house with the girls. Then I came hunting you."

It gave her a warm fuzzy feeling deep down to know that Cody had been that anxious about her. Stacey couldn't remember the last time a person had shown any concern about her whereabouts or worried if anything had happened to her. No man since her first stepfather had shown that much emotion for her and in the end he hadn't either. "I'm sorry I scared you. I hadn't seen Boston and so I thought today was a good day to do so."

"Why didn't you say anything to me about going?"

She hesitated a moment. "I didn't want you to feel pressured to go with me. The girls have just gotten home. I knew you would want to spend time with them. And I know you don't want them to know about us."

"I don't think they need to know we're sleeping together. And about that..." He kicked the door closed and walked her backward as he looked around. "By the way, where's your bedroom? I've missed having you beneath me."

"Do you think that's a good idea?"

"Probably not." He gave her a hot, wet kiss that made his intentions clear.

She gripped his shoulders and returned his kiss. Her center throbbed with need for him. No, it was probably not a good idea but she couldn't help herself. She would worry about how to recover from leaving Cody later. Right now she was going to enjoy every sweet moment she would have with him.

He pulled her hard against him, his desire long and ridged between them. "See how I've missed you."

She pulled back and said as seriously as she could, "You have? You only saw me yesterday."

Cody continued walking her backward as he nuzzled her neck. "Shut up. You know what I mean," he growled. "Now, where is your bed? I need you."

"I like the way you're showing me how much." She wiggled against him, making him moan as she gave him better access to her neck. Her hand slid between them to run along his hot, hard length.

"Stacey, as much as I enjoy trading quips with you, I'd much rather be doing something more meaningful."

She leaned back, giving him an innocent smile and batting her eyelashes. "And you have what in mind?"

He groaned. "You're doing it again." He backed her against the wall. Leaning in, he kissed her passionately before his hand skimmed up over her thigh and slipped beneath the hem of the T-shirt. "I'd hoped for something softer for you but I'm good here."

She giggled. "I like it when it's hard."

Cody groaned as he pressed her more securely to the wall and his lips found hers. He dipped a finger under her panties, making her jerk as he entered her. "There's that sassy mouth again."

She closed her eyes to savor the moment. This was the Cody she would miss the most.

Cody finished the last of his cheese omelet then put his plate down on the planks of Stacey's small porch. They were sitting in her swing with the only light coming from a lamp inside. He raised both hands above his head and took a large, very satisfying stretch. Done, he gave a little nudge with his toe and started the swing. He had no idea that he could be so…happy.

When had he last thought of happiness? Years? Obligations, his job, his girls, those, yes. The shoulds, musts and need-tos of his life—yes. But happiness? That hadn't entered his mind in so long he wasn't sure he could have put a name to it until this moment. Yet wasn't he fooling himself here? As good as he felt now, he knew he'd feel equally bad when Stacey left. She shifted where she sat cross-legged beside him, finishing her meal.

"Thanks for the omelet."

"No problem. You got the extent of my culinary skills. And my refrigerator. You were lucky I had eggs and cheese."

"I noticed things were kind of sparse in there." He took her plate and set it on top of his.

She laid her head against his upper arm. "I've never

kept much because I don't cook for myself often and since I'm leaving tomorrow I was trying to use up what I do have."

A lump formed in his chest. There went his happiness at the reminder she was leaving. Cody watched her. Could he let her go? Did he have a choice? What if he asked her to stay? Would she? He studied Stacey a moment. She looked so amazing with her disordered hair, her make-up-free face and dressed in what he'd learned was one of his T-shirts. He was such a lovesick calf. "Have you ever thought about staying in one place?" He held his breath, waiting for her answer. Maybe, just maybe she would answer as he hoped.

"I did one time but it didn't work out." She stated it as a fact, lacking emotion.

His heart fell. "What happened?"

"My fiancé left me for his old girlfriend a month before the wedding." Her voice sounded hollow, devoid of all emotion. Would she speak of him that way one day? That idea cut like a knife.

Now he had a better idea of why she moved around so much. She'd been hurt. Badly. They were more alike than he'd given her credit for when they'd first met. He'd run from his troubles in California and she was running around the world to hide from hers. "It was his loss."

Stacey stood and looked down at him in the dim light. "Thanks for saying that. A girl likes to hear things like that. Okay, no more talk about the past or the future. Right now is all I'm interested in."

He sighed. He could refuse her so little. He'd been kidding himself for days. This had to come to an end. It might kill him when Stacey got on the ferry but he wouldn't give up what time they could still share.

She clasped his hand, tugged him up and led him into the house. This time her eyes shone bright with seduction and desire. She led him to the bedroom he couldn't find earlier. They removed the few clothes they wore, saying nothing, just looking into each other's eyes. Their love-making was deliberate, delicious and passionately deep. Everything about it said they were aware this would be their last time together.

Sometime later Stacey asked while Cody was dressing, "May I come over and say bye to Jean and Lizzy tomorrow? I'm planning to take the midafternoon ferry off the island. I don't want to just disappear on them. I had that happen to me more than once and I won't do it to them."

He looked at her, indecision obvious in his eyes. "Why don't you come for a late breakfast?" Cody asked as he buckled his belt.

"I don't think that would be a good idea." It would surely make it more difficult for her.

"At this point nothing about this is going to be easy."

She couldn't disagree with that statement.

"The girls would really like to be with you for a while one last time." What he left off was how he would feel about it.

He put his hands on each side of her where she lay on the bed and gave her a long tender kiss. "I'll say my goodbye now. It has been nice knowing you, Stacey. Good luck."

Stacey didn't like the sound of finality in his voice. Cody was already distancing himself. She didn't want that. Not yet. She reached around his neck and tried to pull him down to her but he stayed propped on his palms above her. He gave her one more searching look. As if he were memorizing her. He straightened. She groaned her complaint.

"I've got to go. I still feel guilty about lying to the sitter."

She stretched like a cat in the sun, arching her back so that her breasts were thrust high into his chest.

Cody muttered a word under his breath that wasn't repeatable in polite company. "You aren't playing fair."

Stacey pretended to giggle, trying to lighten the mood. "Is there a problem, Doc?"

"Yeah, there is." With that he turned on his heel and left.

Her smile dropped and she looked at the empty doorway. She had a problem too. Oh, yes, she would leave part of herself on Maple Island. A part she was sure she would never recover.

When she arrived at Cody's the next morning she was confident the idea of her having a meal with his family was a wrong step but she'd agreed to do it and wouldn't turn away. For once in her life she was willing to chuck out her major rule in life and not make sure she had said her goodbyes. It would have been so much easier to just get on the ferry and not look back. But she couldn't bring herself to do that.

Jean and Lizzy were giddy with excitement over seeing her. As Cody once again cooked pancakes, each girl took turns to share stories about their trip with their grandparents. They also got out the things they had brought home with them. A rock, a pine cone, a special cup, and every one Stacey treated as if it were made of gold.

Stacey presented the girls with the book she had bought them. They were happy to get it, even wanting her to read it to them. She did so while Cody continued to work on the food. She shared the inscription she'd written on the inside cover: "'To two very special girls. I'll always hold you and our time together in my heart.'"

They wouldn't understand that at their young ages but they would as adults. Maybe they would think about her when they read it to their own children. Wherever she was, it would be nice to think someone was thinking about her on occasion.

She looked at Cody after she'd read it. He was watching them with shadowy eyes. What feelings was he hiding there? Did he think it was too much? He'd been cool, even standoffish when she had arrived.

He seemed as resigned to her leaving as she was determined she would go. That was good. She didn't want a scene. There shouldn't be one anyway—she had told him all along that she wouldn't be staying. Why she was even worrying about it, she didn't know. Not once had he suggested that she should stay. There was no job here for her now. Cody had certainly not offered her a position in his life.

They'd had their fun and games while they'd had the chance and now it was over. They could part as friends and their time together would be a nice interlude she'd remember fondly. Sadly, despite trying to pretend, she wasn't sure it would be that simple for her.

Cody looked across the table at Jean and Lizzy. They were growing up fast. Right now they were all smiles and lively conversation, each one trying to talk over the other in an effort to hold Stacey's attention. She, as always, was listening raptly to each word. She would make a wonderful mother.

He had to stop that line of thought. It would get him nowhere. He wasn't even sure he could offer anyone that role ever again. Bringing her into their life permanently was another issue completely but, heaven help him, he would ache for her for a long time to come.

Cody had to stop himself more than once from holding her hand under the table. He just wanted to touch her for as long as possible. Instead, he resisted and tried to keep the meal moving on a light note.

It wasn't until they were all through with their meals that the atmosphere became gloomy. Stacey reached across the table and took the hands of Jean and Lizzy. "I wanted to come here today to tell you both I was leaving this afternoon."

The girls' smiles dropped.

"Can't you stay longer?" Lizzy asked mournfully.

Stacey's lips drew into a thin line and she shook her head slightly. "No. Remember I told you that I have a job waiting for me. They need me."

"But who is going to help us with our dance costumes? Daddy is no good at it." Jean looked from her to him and back again.

Stacey glanced at Cody giving him a weak smile before her attention returned to the girls. "Maybe you can use your imaginations and help him."

This was just what Cody had tried to guard against. Once again someone Jean and Lizzy cared about would no longer be in their lives. He'd been unable to stay away from Stacey and now Lizzy and Jean were caught in the fallout.

"But we like you," Lizzy announced.

"And I like you both too. Me leaving won't change that."

"Do you have to go today?" Jean asked.

"I do. My mother is expecting me for a visit and then I'm off to Ethiopia." Stacey sounded as if she was trying to put an excited note in her words but it was falling flat.

The girls' eyes glistened with tears.

"Will you come back?" Jean asked.

Cody was devastated. This was the daughter who had taken time to warm up to Stacey and now that she had, Stacey was leaving. This was far worse than he'd imagined. He had to defuse the conversation. "Girls, we want to wish Stacey well, don't we? So let's smile and be happy for her. Since you have finished eating, how about putting your dishes in the sink. It's a nice day so why don't you go outside and play? Stacey doesn't have to leave for a little while. She can come out and say a final goodbye later."

As the girls scrambled to do as he'd asked, Stacey gave him a resigned look. "I didn't think it would be this hard. Never has been before." She said the words more to herself than to him.

Neither one of them said anything for a few minutes.

His phone ringing interrupted the silence. "I've got to get that."

Stacey nodded.

Cody picked his phone up off the counter and went into the next room to talk.

"Dr. Brennan," Cody answered. He hoped he didn't have to go in. He wanted all the time he could get with Stacey, even if it was rocky.

"Cody, it's Marsha Lewiston."

His clinical nurse. The one Stacey had been filling in for. "Marsha, it's good to hear from you. I'm looking forward to having you back tomorrow." That wasn't exactly accurate. If Marsha was his nurse again then Stacey would be gone. The knot that had formed in his stomach grew. "How's your mother doing?'

"That's the thing, Cody. She's recovering well from the surgery but she isn't getting any younger. I know this is short notice but I'm going to resign my position. I need to live and work closer to Mom."

Cody couldn't miss the extra thump of his heart at Marsha's announcement. There would be an opening for Stacey to stay. "I understand. You have to do what's best for you and your mother. I will miss working with you."

"I'll make it a formal note by email in the morning."

"That sounds fine. Let me know if you need a reference. I assure you it will be a glowing one."

"Thanks, Cody. I appreciate that. Again, I'm sorry for not saying something sooner."

"Don't worry about it." As far as Cody was concerned, the timing was perfect. He could offer Stacey the position. Maybe it would give her an excuse to stay. They could build from there.

CHAPTER NINE

WITH HIS PHONE call completed Cody returned to the kitchen, hope making his step lighter. There he found Stacey standing at the sink, doing the dishes.

"Leave those. I'll do them later." Cody moved around the counter near her and leaned a hip against it.

"I don't mind. It gives me something to do." She placed a plate into the dishwasher. "I have to go in a few minutes anyway."

He tried to tamp down the excitement that Marsha's phone call had generated in him. Would Stacey go for it? He couldn't help but be thrilled about the idea. Maybe it would be enough to get her to stay longer. Still, he wasn't clear on how he really felt about Stacey agreeing to what he was about to ask. Would she see it as him asking for more between them?

The fear that something he couldn't get back was leaving his life enveloped him and helped him make up his mind. He had to ask her. He couldn't let her go without at least trying to get her to stay on some kind of terms. Even if right now it was for work reasons.

"That was Marsha. You know, the nurse that you've been filling in for. She has decided to hand in her resignation."

Stacey stopped in mid-motion, the dishcloth dangling in her hand, to look at him.

"Effective tomorrow. She wants to work closer to her aging mother." He smiled at her. "It looks like I have an opening for a good clinical nurse." His eyes searched her face. "Interested?"

Time hung, unmoving. Cody's eyes searched her face. Stacey said nothing. Panic burned through him. Acid rose in his throat. She was taking too long to answer for it to go his way.

With a sad look in her eyes, Stacey finally shook her head slowly. "Cody, I can't. I've already committed to the job in Ethiopia."

"Can't or won't?"

"I told you when we first met that I don't stay in one place long. That's just not who I am. Let's not make this into something unpleasant after what we have shared. We both knew when we got together it was just for fun. Would only last for a few days."

"I thought that's what you would say." He had to admit he was disappointed but he'd known her view before he'd asked the question. Cody couldn't help himself; he had to know. He stepped closer to her and asked in a low flat voice, "When you leave here, you won't look back, will you?"

Her eyes filled with pain and uncertainty. Her lips thinned and she shook her head. "Cody, I told you how I am. Let's not ruin what we've had."

Cody hated the idea that she could leave him and that he'd mean nothing more to her than some man she'd met and bedded while on Maple Island. He wanted her to care more than that. "What have we had, Stacey? Just sex? What exactly?"

"Isn't that what we agreed to? What you wanted? I don't remember you offering me more."

"Yeah, but I had the impression that it might be more than that now." He shouldn't have let himself get involved deeply enough that his heart hurt at the thought of never seeing her again. Why hadn't he protected himself more? If she really cared for him and the girls, she would want to stay. At least try taking the job. He tamped down the anger that welled in him.

Getting frustrated with Stacey would only make the situation worse. Why didn't she act as if she was hurting over her choice to leave as much as he was? She was just like Rachael after all. Only cared about herself.

Stacey hadn't counted on there being this much emotional baggage when she left. It had never existed before. When she had become physically involved with Cody she'd feared this might happen but had never considered it would be like carrying a car around on her back. Yet she was determined to put a smile on her face and soldier on. Just because there was a job opening at the clinic, it didn't mean that she was going to dump all her plans and stay here.

Anyway, given some space, these developing feelings for Cody would probably pass. They had when her fiancé had left her, as well as her stepfather. Now she could talk about those times without even flinching. Given enough time, she would be able to treat thoughts of Cody with the same disregard. She would move on. That's what she did. Kept moving.

She was kidding herself. This time it was different. She would tie all the sweet memories of Cody and their time together with a pink bow in her mind and take them out to pore over every day forever. She almost groaned out loud.

He studied her a moment. "You know, you are the last person I'd have sworn I would ever think this about, but you really are a coward, aren't you?"

She dropped the dishcloth into the sink and rounded on him. Her face flushed. How dared he! "What?"

"You are scared."

"What are you talking about?" Stacey considered herself fearless. She had lived in the jungle, the desert and places with no running water. She wasn't afraid of anything.

"You can't even live in the same place for more than a few months at a time because you're afraid you might care about someone. So what's the plan? Live in fear all your life?"

"You have real gall to say that to me when you have closed yourself off on an island? You have some nerve." For a second he felt as if she had struck him.

He bared his teeth. "You don't know the hell that I…" he pointed outside "…and my girls have lived through. I can't just open the door and let *anyone* in."

"No, I don't know what you have been through but what I do know is that you can't put your life on hold because you are afraid of it happening again. Somehow you're going to have to learn to let go enough to let people in and, when they're old enough, let your girls go. When I got here you were so closed off that I was afraid if you smiled your face would crumble. You couldn't even take a joke!"

"I let *you* in!"

"You did." She shook her head. "But only enough to have sex with me. I was easy, though." She raised her hand to stop him from speaking. "Not that kind of easy. Easy for you because I was only going to be here for a month. That way you didn't have to give too much of yourself or make a commitment. I was a safe bet. You didn't have to worry about me being the wrong choice because you knew I wasn't going to stay around." She harrumphed. "I was both the right and wrong choice. Right for a fling and wrong for you in the long haul. Which made me perfect." She chuckled dryly.

"Why do you think you're wrong for me for the long haul?"

"For starters, I don't know anything about being a mother. I probably had one of the worst. She spent all her time worrying about keeping her man or getting the next one. I mostly raised myself. You need a woman who would be attentive to your girls. I don't know how to do that."

He pointed toward the table. "That's bull. I just watched you with them a few minutes ago. And when you were helping them with their costumes. You're a natural. That's just one more of your excuses."

"You told me once you wanted a marriage like your parents have and hadn't got it. That doesn't mean it isn't out there for you. The right woman will come along. You just have to open up enough to let her in." The idea of Cody having another woman permanently in his life made Stacey almost lose her breakfast.

"Now you're giving me marriage advice," he stated incredulously. "The woman who won't stay in one place long enough to have a relationship. That's laughable." But he wasn't laughing.

"You are right. I have no business telling you how to run your life. Really I don't."

His shoulders slumped as if he were defeated. "I grew up believing marriage was forever. Permanent. Then addiction destroyed it all. Now I'm gun-shy. Afraid to trust or believe in anyone. Particularly where the girls are concerned."

He paused and looked lost for a moment. Under any other circumstances she would have felt sorry for him. A stricken look had come over his face and he straightened as if he were ready to go to battle. "But I'll have you know I don't lightly invite people into my life or my girls'. I took a chance with you."

If she'd let herself admit it, she knew she wanted what Cody offered. All of it. But she couldn't take it. History told her that it would be snatched from her just when she started to feel secure. She couldn't take that chance. Stacey's voice softened. "I know you did. Only because you knew I would soon be leaving."

Cody had had enough. What had started out as a job offer had turned into an ugly personal argument. "All I'm saying is that if you take my job offer then we could explore what's between us. Maybe I could let go some, trust more. Trust you. But you'd have to stop running. Could you do that? Let me in enough that you could trust me not to leave you? Look around you. You've made friends here, have a job you say you love. The girls and I are here. Why can't you accept you're good enough to deserve all of that?"

"Maybe because I've never felt wanted before and I don't know how to handle it!"

Cody stepped closer to her. There was a plea in his voice when he said, "I could help you."

"Yeah. I know how that goes. You'd have me around

until I do something you don't think is right. Then you'd not want me anymore. You'd leave me or I'd have to leave!" She shook her head as if she was trying to dislodge the past. "No, I can't. I won't go through that again. I won't be left behind again. Ever."

"I would never do that to you." Cody reached for her but she backed away, out of touching distance.

If she allowed him to touch her, she'd never be able to leave. "You left your wife. Why wouldn't you leave me?"

Air whistled from Cody as if he had just been sucker-punched. "I stayed to the bitter end. I didn't want to give up. I was just left no choice."

"You say I ran away. But you have run in your own way as much as I have. You've moved all the way across the country to get away."

"To protect my children. My move from California was different from hopping from place to place around the world because you're scared to give anyone or any-place a chance."

Stacey scowled at him. "That's not true."

He cocked his head and gave her a narrowed-eyed look. "Are you sure about that? Are you happy with your life? Being alone all the time?"

She flinched.

"You do know you don't have to go." He let the words sink in.

She stepped toward him. "I have already made a commitment."

He met her glare head on. "Yeah, but I also offered you one here. With me." That sounded too close to a proposal.

"To be your nurse and your night-time booty call whenever the girls happen to be elsewhere. Sounds like the perfect life for you."

That time she'd cut him to the core. Even to him it sounded one-sided. Sleazy and self-centered.

"Daddy, why're you and Stacey fighting?" came Lizzy's small voice from the doorway.

She and Cody whirled in her direction in shock. He hoped Lizzy hadn't heard Stacey's last statement.

Stacey went down on one knee and brought Lizzy into her arms. "Your daddy and I were just talking. I was telling him it's time for me to go now." She looked over Lizzy's shoulder at Cody. "How about a big hug before I do?"

Lizzy had a sad little smile on her face.

"Bye, sweetheart." Stacey pulled her close.

Standing, Stacey moved toward the back door. "I'm going to speak to Jean on the way out. Bye, Cody." She gave him a little wave.

His lips drew into a thin line and he closed his eyes. When he opened them she was gone.

CHAPTER TEN

CODY HAD BEEN working through his pain and loneliness. Not well, but he tried. The days since Stacey had left had been long and seemingly endless as the ocean he spent too much time looking out at. The nights made the days feel short and sweet. Without Stacey next to him he couldn't rest. When he did sleep, he dreamed of her. He was just existing and didn't know how to come out of the fog. His heart was broken and Stacey was the only cure.

The day she had left and his back door had closed between them he'd been confident that all the joy in his life had gone out that door with her. He'd not been wrong.

Nothing about living whilst being deprived of Stacey was easy. In fact, it made what he'd lived through earlier in his life seem stress-free. He was tied in a knot with no idea how to unsnarl it. Somehow he had to recover from Stacey. Help his girls do so as well.

They spoke of her almost daily, which only increased his pain. Stacey had made such a strong impression on them in such a short time. To make matters worse, he was grumbling at the girls. He was muddling through life and doing a very poor job of even that. The happiness he'd been so surprised to have was gone now. He hadn't been able to hang on to it. Having so briefly tasted it, the loss of it was almost too much for him to bear.

He went through the motions of working. Most of his medical care was done by rote. Nothing interested him. Each patient had become a case instead of a person. The fact that he was doing it all on little or no sleep didn't make matters any better.

The nurses already on staff were taking turns filling Stacey's position. They were efficient enough but there was no real rapport between them and him. He missed Stacey's humor, the way she anticipated his next move or need. Heck, he missed her in his professional life almost as much as he did in his private one. She had managed to permeate every corner of his world. He'd been caught up in the tsunami that was Stacey and it was now tossing him around.

Two weeks after Stacey had left he passed the day care as Alex exited.

"Hey, buddy, you got a minute to talk?" Alex asked, putting a hand on Cody's shoulder.

"Uh…sure." Cody wasn't fit company for anyone. "Is there a problem?"

"I think so, but you'll have to confirm it."

That was a cryptic remark for the usually straight-forward Alex. "Is something up with a patient?" Cody couldn't think of who it might be.

"Let's go to my office." They entered and Alex said, "Close the door."

Cody did so then slumped into a chair in front of Alex's desk. "What's going on?"

Alex continued around the desk to sit behind it. "That's just what I was going to ask you."

"What do you mean?" Had Alex noticed what a mess his life had become now that Stacey was gone?

"Come on, Cody, you're talking to me. Neither one of us has any dirty laundry that the other doesn't already know about. Something's eating at you. You've not been yourself since Stacey left." Cody started to deny it but Alex raised his hand. "Don't say there wasn't something between you because this is a small island and an even smaller clinic."

"Great. I thought I was covering better than that," Cody muttered.

"Sorry to disappoint you, buddy. So what happened?"

A big fat fight. Too much said. Too little said. Not the right things said. Cody shrugged. "Nothing. It was time for her to leave and she did."

"Did you want her to stay?" Alex watched him closely.

Cody hated to admit how much. "Sure I did. I offered her Marsha's job but she said no."

Alex nodded his head a few times and pursed his lips. "You offered her a job. I see."

Sitting a little straighter, Cody asked, "What do you mean by that?"

"Well, if I have learned anything from Maggie it's that a woman wants more than just a job offer from her man. Did you tell her you loved her?"

He hadn't even dared to think in that vein. If he did he might fall down the hole of despair and never come back out again. It took him a few seconds to answer. "No."

"You do, though, don't you?"

There he was on the edge of the hole. Did he? Yeah, he did. Why had it taken this conversation to make him admit it to himself? Because it was the first time he'd ever really loved a woman enough that he couldn't live without her. He'd never felt that way before.

"I know what it's like to start again. The fear of opening your heart again. It's scary but you need to know, from what I learned about Stacey she has a huge heart and she's nothing like Rachael. From what I saw she was a better mother to Jean and Lizzy in just a few weeks than their biological mother was, can be or ever will be. That said, I need you in top working order around here."

Cody squared his shoulders. "Are you questioning my ability to do my job?"

"Never. I'm questioning whether or not you can survive if you continue like this." Alex leaned forward. "Right now, I don't think you're functioning well enough to make sound medical decisions." He frowned briefly and then continued. "Maggie and I had a hard trail to walk and we came out on the other side. I think you will too. Have you thought about going after Stacey? Telling her how you feel? Maybe offering her a ring instead of a job?"

"She's in Ethiopia," Cody said flatly.

Alex leaned toward him, pinning him with a look. "You fly, don't you? If you don't do something soon, I'm going to have to buy you out of the clinic because your sad face is starting to affect the morale around here. All I'm saying is think about it."

Cody did, for every hour of the day. Nothing Alex had said could Cody refute. He had been happy. Life had been good with Stacey in it. She had added to his life, not taken away, like Rachael had. The girls were crazy about her. He was too—heck, he was in love with her.

Was he really still letting Rachael control his life? He might have moved three thousand miles away from her yet what she had done governed every decision he made. Stacey had been right. It was time he let go. Trusted somebody. Admit that he could have that dream of a true partnership within a marriage, just with a different person. He hoped that person would be Stacey. It was finally time to move on with his life.

Just as shameful, he had looked down on Stacey for her lifestyle and had accused her of being a coward. He'd taken the high road of superiority in the knowledge that he had established a home. Living here on the island, he might not have been physically running, but what he'd been doing was certainly running emotionally. Never dating, never taking an interest in a woman, never opening up to someone. Until Stacey. He had let a destroyed dream and guilt rule his life for too long. His narrow world had become all about his girls and trying to protect them from life. What a horrible example to set for Jean and Lizzy.

Happiness was what he should be encouraging them to strive for. He'd had that with Stacey. Somehow he was going to get it back. The question now was how.

When Stacey had left Cody's house that Sunday, she'd gone back to her cottage and picked up her already packed bag. She'd made her way to the ferry in time to take an earlier one. There had been no one there to wave goodbye to. That had only added to her sadness.

She'd sat in the corner of the sparsely populated boat, not even looking out the window. Every fiber of her being had begged to stay but her mind had told her no. It wasn't to be. Nothing about her life was truly different than it had been before she'd come to Maple Island.

She had changed her plane reservation and ended up

at her mother's door sooner than expected. The second the door to her mother's apartment had opened, Stacey had fallen into her arms. She had clung to her mother like she was the lifeline she was. Stacey's heart was broken and she'd run home. Regardless of the fact her mother's own life was so screwed up, she still remained the only constant in Stacey's. That evening she'd told her mother she was tired and had gone to bed early.

The next morning she'd woken in a small bedroom in her mother's apartment to the sounds of cars driving by, the trash truck banging and clanging, and people yelling through the open windows. She wasn't in paradise anymore.

This wasn't Maple Island, where the seagulls squawked as they fought over breakfast in the rolling waves and the sun shone warmly on her face. The one spot in all the world where Cody was, where his loving was so sweet it was almost painful. The place she'd chosen to leave behind.

She'd rolled over, burying her face in a pillow, and groaned. How had it come to this?

After their first kiss she'd never doubted it would be a difficult parting between her and Cody. Even knowing that, she'd never dreamed they wouldn't at least part friends. She couldn't believe she'd left with such ugliness between them. For all the wonderful memories she had stored away, those unpleasant few moments of their final fight tarnished them.

There was a knock on the bedroom door. Her mother asked, "Stacey, may I come in?"

"I guess so." There was no enthusiasm in her response. She sounded wretched even to her own ears.

Her mother came to sit on the bed like she used to do

when Stacey had been a child. "You've been here a day and hardly gotten out of bed. I think it's time we talked."

Stacey knew that was true. She needed to understand things about her mother so she could reconcile her own beliefs. Cody had made her question them. Had she really been running all these years? Fearful of feeling anything for someone? Scared of being left? Stacey didn't want to live like that any longer. She wanted security and love. To feel special to someone. She wanted what she had lost with Cody.

"You get a shower and I'll fix us some pancakes and you can tell me what has you so out of sorts." This wasn't a request from her mother but a directive.

Left with no choice, Stacey crawled out of bed and headed for the tiny bath. She stood under the water until it turned cold.

There was a sharp rap on the door. "Pancakes in five."

Pancakes. She'd loved Cody's pancakes. Could see him standing at the stove, grinning, as he flipped one perfectly...

Stacey dressed, and with her hair still twisted in a towel she went to her mother's small galley kitchen. She took a seat at the two-person table next to a window overlooking a street with a few trees. Once again she longed for Maple Island.

They ate in silence. Mostly her mother ate. When her mother finished she placed her fork on her plate with a loud ping. Stacey jumped.

"Okay, spill."

Stacey fingered the bracelet Jean and Lizzy had given her. She rarely took it off. "I've been working for this doctor. He has two small girls."

"Aw, I suspected as much. This is about a man. He's

gotten to you. I was wondering when you would finally let it happen."

Cody *had* gotten to her. Enough so that her entire world had tilted. She didn't know how to right it. "We got close, had an argument and then it was time for me to leave."

Her mother watched her closely. "There's more to it than that."

Her mom had always been able to read her expressions. Stacey hadn't realized that until this moment. She had believed her mother was oblivious to her and her feelings. Now she questioned whether or not she'd given her mother enough credit. "Do you mind if I ask you something?"

Her mother got up and poured them more tea then sat again. "What do you want to know?"

"Why couldn't you hold a marriage together?"

Her mother flinched then put her elbows on the table, holding the warm tea mug between her hands. "I don't know. Maybe because I was always searching for something from some man that he wasn't able to give me." She shrugged. "Or it might be that I can't open up enough to really let someone in. That I'm afraid they might see the real me and not like it. I know I've hurt you with my failed marriages. Your father, then your stepfather. I could see you missed him terribly. I hated myself for making you go through that."

"So your answer was to take me away from my friends as well by moving to Miami?" Some of Stacey's spirit had returned.

"That wasn't my best decision. I was running from the bill collectors."

Stacey had had no idea. She had to give her mom some sympathy there.

"I can't change what happened but what I can tell you is that if you ever find a man that you believe you can give your heart and soul to, and you know he can do the same to you, then grasp him and hold on for all your life. That's a precious thing that I've never had and wish desperately I could find. Don't let my abysmal track record spoil your happiness."

"It's still not too late for you." Stacey reached over and put her hand over her mother's. This type of heart-to-heart they had never had. Suddenly she felt sorry for her mother. Stacey had shared more with Cody in a few weeks than her mother had found in her lifetime with her various partners.

"Maybe not. The question is, have you found someone you could settle down with? Tell me about this doctor."

Stacey shared with her mother all about Cody and Jean and Lizzy, and Maple Island. The memories of their times together returned sweet and clear. Stacey finished with, "We had a huge fight. I had to leave and I won't see them again. I have a job in Ethiopia."

Her mother gave her a thoughtful look. "Do you love Cody?"

How like her mother to cut straight to the point. Stacey's eyes didn't waver as she answered, "With all my heart."

"Then do something about it."

"He offered me a job but said nothing about how he felt. I'm obligated to go to Ethiopia. After our fight I'm not sure he even wants to speak to me, let alone be willing to wait for me to come back."

"Then you need to decide if he's worth fighting for.

Can you live without him? Probably. Will you be happy, though?" She shrugged.

Her mother still searched for what Stacey was confident she had already found with Cody. He and the girls had captured her heart. She would meet her obligation in Ethiopia until they could find a replacement for her. Then she would make arrangements to return to Maple Island. She intended to find out if Cody loved her as well.

Cody was coming out of surgery when Alex stopped him. "Do you have a sec?"

After their conversation two weeks earlier, Cody had taken hold of his emotions and stuffed them away in an effort to get his life back into line. He had called the agency that Stacey worked for and had been told that she was no longer employed by them. She had left no forwarding address. She had just disappeared. No, it was more like he had let her go.

Now he was only surviving because of the girls. Each day he hoped that Stacey might write and he would have a lead to what village she was working in in Ethiopia. It had been a month since she had left and every day he was disappointed when he looked through the mail. Somehow he had to find a way to contact her.

"Since you're not taking any interest in hiring a new clinical nurse and I'm worried about overworking the nurses we have, I've taken the liberty of having a staffing service set up a few interviews for you. The first one comes in today at three." With that, Alex walked away.

How like Alex to drop something like that in his lap when Cody least expected it. He had dawdled about replacing Stacey because it meant she was gone for good if he filled the position. He had been holding out for her return. He wanted her back in his professional life but more than that he wanted her in his private one as well.

That afternoon Cody was in his office. He picked up the phone. He had time to call one more nursing agency. He'd been working through a list of them, trying to find someone that knew something about Stacey. He'd already tried her cellphone and the number was no longer working. He'd even gone on social media and found nothing. "May I speak to someone who would know something about nurses assigned to Ethiopia?"

"I could probably help you with that information," came a voice he heard nightly in his dreams. *Stacey!*

Cody's head jerked toward the door. His heart clogged his throat. Was she actually here or was he just imagining it because he wanted it so desperately?

She smiled but there was still an unsure look in her eyes. "I'm here for a job interview."

He hung up the phone without saying another word and just stared at her. She was the most beautiful sight he'd ever seen. The simple pink dress she wore accentuated her coloring and her curves. It was demure while at the same time enticing. Her hair hung freely around her shoulders, bouncing with healthiness. His fingers tingled with the desire to run the silkiness through them. She wore the bracelet his daughters had given her on her wrist. Where had she come from? Had Alex put her up to this? He stood. "Hi, Stacey."

"Hello, Cody."

With great effort he stopped himself from circling the desk and scooping her up into his arms. What if that wasn't what she wanted? Maybe she just wanted the job but not him. That thought made him almost double over in pain. He'd said some nasty things to her the day she'd left. Yet here she was, interviewing for a job that would mean she would be working with him almost daily.

"How have you been?" With effort he kept his voice level, professional.

"Busy. I quit my job with the travel nursing agency but still made a short trip to Ethiopia to work until a replacement could be found. I've decided to try staying in one place for a while. I saw on the clinic website there was a job still open here, so I applied for it."

"Did Alex know it was you?" He'd never forgive the man for not putting him out of his misery as soon as he knew it was Stacey coming for the interview.

"Nope. At least, not until I saw him in the hall. He said something peculiar. Something about being damn tired of running a place for lonely hearts."

Cody chuckled. Alex was no doubt fed up with dealing with him and also having Salty unhappy about Mrs. Kerridge-Bates. Love hadn't run smoothly for them either, but at least they had finally sorted out their issues and had admitted to loving each other. They were even planning their wedding. Now, if he could just convince Stacey that they should go down the same path...

"So what makes you want to work at Maple Island Clinic?"

Her mouth quirked. "Do you conduct all your interviews standing up?"

"Uh...no, sorry. Come in and have a seat." She came in and closed the door, then took the chair in front of his desk.

Cody sat as well, clutching his hands in his lap. If he didn't touch her soon, he would die. Yet if he did, it might scare her off. She looked so cool and collected. As if she were unaffected by the weeks that had passed since they had seen one another.

"In answer to your question, you do."

"I do what?" He'd forgotten what he'd asked. She giggled. He loved that sound.

"You asked me why I wanted to work at the clinic and I said because of you."

Did he dare to hope? "Why is that?"

"Because you're the most amazing, giving and caring doctor and man that I know. You are a wonderful father, a good friend and most of all I want to be around you. Working with you would make me a better nurse and person."

Cody's heart swelled. Did she really believe that? He stood and circled the desk then sat on the corner of it within touching distance of her. "You do know that if you take this job, you would be a permanent staff member. Are you prepared to stay here for a lifetime?"

"I am." Her eyes didn't waver.

He gaze didn't leave hers. "I can be demanding, and misguided, and sometimes say things I regret. Can you deal with that?"

"I believe so. I often do the same thing." She continued to hold his gaze. Stacey had the most amazing green eyes.

"It sounds like we could get along well together." He knew exactly how well they could get along and wanted them to find that happiness again. "Do you have any questions for me?"

"I do have one." She looked down.

He waited. Was she afraid to ask him? Now, that was unlike the Stacey he knew.

Her eyes met his again. "Do you love me as much as I love you?"

His heart raced, his hands shook as he lifted her out of the chair and crushed her to him. He kissed her with all the passion that had built inside him while they'd been apart. It flowed freely over the dam he'd created to try to protect himself. She returned his kisses with the same abandon. He now had everything he wanted in life in his arms and he was going to do whatever it took to keep her there.

"I missed you so much. I've called everywhere, looking for you." He nibbled at her neck.

"Cody?"

"Yes?" He continued to kiss her eyes, her nose and her cheeks. He inhaled the peach smell he couldn't get enough of.

"You didn't answer my question." There was a hint of uncertainty in her voice.

He leaned away until he could meet her eyes. "I love you too. More than life."

Stacey lay in Cody's bed that evening, wrapped in his arms. Life took odd turns and sometimes gave a person something they never dreamed was possible. That had happened for her. She had what she had hoped for all her life—someone to love her, a place to call home and a man who would never leave her. Could her life get much better?

"Hey, what're you thinking about over there?"

"About how happy I am."

Cody rolled to her, placing a kiss on her bare shoulder. "You make me happy."

She cupped his cheek. "I'm sorry I said all those mean things to you."

"Don't be. I needed to hear them. You were right.

That's why the girls are at my parents' and I'm here. I have to start letting go."

"I'm proud of you. What you said to me hit home as well. I talked to my mother, really talked. She's the one who convinced me to come and see you, to tell you how I felt. It turns out that in some ways she's been a good mother. I just didn't want to see it."

"It sounds like we have both made steps in the right direction." He gave her a tender kiss. Pulling away, he said, "It's about time for the girls to call. They'll be so excited to see you but they might ask questions we don't want to answer if we don't put some clothes on."

Not long after that Stacey could hear Cody already talking to the girls before she came out of the bathroom. They were video-chatting. She stepped up behind him and smiled into the screen at the two girls that she loved almost as much as she did their daddy.

"Hi, Jean. Hi, Lizzy."

"Stacey!" the girls squealed in unison.

"You came back. I knew you would," Jean said with a satisfied smile.

"I'm glad to be back. I missed you both so much. I look forward to hugging you when you get home."

"You're wearing the bracelet we gave you." Lizzy said, pointing.

"I am. I've thought about you both every day we have been apart." She squeezed Cody's shoulder. She'd thought of him every minute.

Cody pushed the chair back and spoke to Stacey. "Why don't you have a seat? I think the girls have something they want to ask you."

Stacey gave him a questioning look but took the spot he had vacated. She looked into the screen at the smiling faces. Cody came round beside her and went down on one knee, taking her hand.

"Okay, girls," Cody said.

"Will you marry us?" all three of them asked at the same time.

Stacey blinked back tears as she looked into Cody's eyes. "I can't think of anything I would love more."

She wrapped her arms around Cody's neck and they kissed to the sound of "Ooh!" coming from the girls.

EPILOGUE

STACEY FLOATED ON happiness like a hot-air balloon through a cloudless July sky. It was her wedding day. *Wedding day.*

Fleur fussed around her, tugging here and adjusting there, as Stacey prepared to walk down Cody's porch steps to the beach where he was waiting. "You look beautiful. I can hardly wait until Cody sees you. Your dress is perfect."

Stacey glanced down at the simple gauzy fabric with the pink ribbon at the waist. She carried a bouquet of pink roses that were a gift from Cody. "Thank you. Just think, you and Rick will be having your wedding day in only a couple of weeks."

Fleur stopped what she was doing. A serene look came over her face, along with a slight smile. She turned to Stacey. "There's nothing like marrying the man you love, is there?"

"No, there isn't." Seconds later the sound of Jean and Lizzy giggling drew her attention. They were coming up the path from the beach.

Jean called, "Stacey, you'd better come. Daddy's getting nervous, he said."

"I was just waiting for you two to escort me." Stacey

went down the steps to meet her future with a bright smile on her face.

"You're so pretty," Lizzy breathed in awe.

"You two look beautiful." The girls wore soft pink matching dresses that flowed in the slight breeze. Matching flowers circled their heads.

Fleur went down the steps carefully. At the bottom she spoke to Stacey. "Give me one minute to tell the guitar player to start playing and then you can come meet the groom." She disappeared between the rocks.

Stacey stepped down the stairs. "Are we ready, girls?"

Jean and Lizzy's faces turned serious as they started back toward the beach. Stacey followed close behind. Notes of the wedding march flowed on the ocean breeze as she stepped between the rocks to see Cody ahead, waiting for her at the end of the lines of chairs that formed an aisle. He had never looked more handsome than he did then, dressed in a light gray suit with a crisp white shirt open at the neck. Alex, his best man, would stand beside him until she joined Cody in front of the pastor then Alex would take a seat next to Fleur.

The girls paused in front of Cody and he kissed the tops of their heads before they went to sit beside his mother and father on the right side front row. Across from them was her mother. She was smiling but her eyes held a glossy look.

When Cody's gaze found hers, Stacey's middle fluttered. He took two steps forward and offered his hand. She grasped it and he brought her to him as they stared into each other's eyes.

The pastor cleared his throat and they guiltily turned to him.

The rest of the ceremony was a blur for Stacey. Before

she knew it Cody was kissing her and they were going
back down the aisle to applause and smiles. They continued until they got to the house. At the bottom of the
steps Cody picked her up and swung her around then let
her slide to her feet. "I love you, Mrs. Brennan."

She was now Mrs. Cody Brennan. Stacey Brennan.
She liked the sound of all of it. "I love you, Dr. Brennan."
She reached up and kissed him.

They climbed the stairs to the porch, where they would
greet their guests before they went inside for the reception. The first to join them were the girls. They came
running. Close behind them were Cody's parents.

"I'm hungry," Lizzy said as she reached them.

She and Cody laughed.

"I'm glad you're going to be our mother." Jean hugged
her.

Stacey returned it tightly. "I am too."

"I'll see about them," his mother said. "This is your
day." She hurried the girls on.

"Congratulations, son," his father said, with a hand-
shake.

Just behind them was her mother. She hugged Stacey then Cody. "I wish you both the best." She looked at
Stacey and smiled.

Soon Rick and Fleur were coming up the stairs, along
with Alex and Maggie. They were all smiles.

After all the congratulations had been offered, Maggie
said to no one in particular, "I'm sorry Rafael and Summer had to miss this but I know they're enjoying their
honeymoon in Spain."

"When they get home, maybe we can all get together
and share wedding pictures," Fleur suggested.

The men groaned.

Stacey's heart expanded. She'd not only gained Cody and the girls but this clinic "family" as well. For someone who had so little family of her own, she now had a lot.

Other members of the Maple Island community stopped to speak on their way inside. Soon she and Cody joined the crowd enjoying food and drinks. The first people they met near the wedding cake were Salty and Philomena.

"Congratulations, Doc." Salty offered his hand to Cody. "The steps were too much for us so we came round to the front door," Salty said in his gravelly voice. Philomena stood beside him, leaning on a decorative silver cane. "I told you a good woman is hard to find."

Philomena gave him a nudge. "Uh…and you found one, too."

Stacey leaned against Cody and squeezed his arm. She enjoyed the look of embarrassment that washed over Salty's face.

Philomena smiled at Stacey. "Beautiful bride and a beautiful wedding. I'm so happy for you both."

"Thank you." Stacey couldn't stop smiling. She looked around at the crowded room. She couldn't believe how much her life had changed in such a short time. For a person who'd had almost nobody in her life, she had now found a home and a community of what would become long-time friends.

Cody tugged her away so that it was only the two of them. He watched her closely. "What're you thinking?"

"Just that you have given me everything I've ever dreamed of and more. I love you so much."

He pulled her tight against him. "You have done exactly the same for me."

* * * * *

LET'S TALK
Romance

For exclusive extracts, competitions
and special offers, find us online:

 facebook.com/millsandboon

 @millsandboonuk

 @millsandboon

Or get in touch on 0844 844 1351*

For all the latest titles coming soon,
visit millsandboon.co.uk/nextmonth

*Calls cost 7p per minute plus your phone company's price per
minute access charge